Reproductive Rights

Other Books of Related Interest

Opposing Viewpoints Series
Feminism
Gender in the 21st Century
Personhood
The #MeToo Movement

At Issue Series
Campus Sexual Violence
Gender Politics
The Politicization of the Supreme Court
Sexual Consent

Current Controversies Series
Are There Two Americas?
LGBTQ Rights
States' Rights and the Role of the Federal Government
Violence Against Women

> "Congress shall make no law … abridging the freedom of speech, or of the press."
>
> *First Amendment to the U.S. Constitution*

The basic foundation of our democracy is the First Amendment guarantee of freedom of expression. The Opposing Viewpoints series is dedicated to the concept of this basic freedom and the idea that it is more important to practice it than to enshrine it.

Reproductive Rights

Sabine Cherenfant, Book Editor

Published in 2023 by Greenhaven Publishing, LLC
2544 Clinton Street,
Buffalo NY 14224

Copyright © 2023 by Greenhaven Publishing, LLC

First Edition

All rights reserved. No part of this book may be reproduced in any form without permission in writing from the publisher, except by a reviewer.

Articles in Greenhaven Publishing anthologies are often edited for length to meet page requirements. In addition, original titles of these works are changed to clearly present the main thesis and to explicitly indicate the author's opinion. Every effort is made to ensure that Greenhaven Publishing accurately reflects the original intent of the authors. Every effort has been made to trace the owners of the copyrighted material.

Cover image: Image Point Fr/Shutterstock.com

Library of Congress CataloginginPublication Data

Names: Cherenfant, Sabine, editor.
Title: Reproductive rights / Sabine Cherenfant, book editor.
Description: First edition. | New York : Greenhaven Publishing, 2023. | Series: Opposing viewpoints | Includes bibliographical references and index. | Audience: Ages 15+ | Audience: Grades 10-12 | Summary: "Anthology of articles and guided reading material exploring the controversial issue of reproductive rights"-- Provided by publisher.
Identifiers: LCCN 2022023636 | ISBN 9781534509160 (library binding) | ISBN 9781534509153 (paperback)
Subjects: LCSH: Reproductive rights--United States--Juvenile literature. | Abortion--Moral and ethical aspects--United States--Juvenile literature.
Classification: LCC HQ766.5.U5 R476 2023 | DDC 362.1988/800973--dc23/eng/20220607
LC record available at https://lccn.loc.gov/2022023636

Manufactured in the United States of America

Website: http://greenhavenpublishing.com

Contents

The Importance of Opposing Viewpoints   11
Introduction   14

Chapter 1: Should Abortions Be Legal?
Chapter Preface   18
1. Criminalizing Abortion Only Makes Abortion Less Safe   19
   Amnesty International
2. The U.S. Abortion Bans Abuse Women's Personal Freedom   28
   Kimberley Brownlee
3. Abortion Is Not the Answer to Gender Inequality   33
   Paul Stark
4. Men Should Not Have Abortion Rights   37
   Marcus Lee
5. When Abortion Is Illegal, Marginalized and Low-Income People Suffer the Most   43
   Prudence Flowers
6. Overturning *Roe* Is Out of Step with Public Opinion   48
   Julie Rovner

Periodical and Internet Sources Bibliography   52

Chapter 2: Is Sex Education a Right?
Chapter Preface   54
1. Planned Parenthood Has Helped Millions of Women   56
   Maureen Miller
2. Four Reasons Why Planned Parenthood Should Be Defunded   62
   Alexandra DeSanctis
3. Why Planned Parenthood Should Be Defunded   67
   Laurence M. Vance

4. Comprehensive Sex Education Can Help Keep
   Children and Teens Safe   73
   Ian Dunt
5. The Role of Education in Preventing
   Sexual Misconduct   79
   Laura McGuire

Periodical and Internet Sources Bibliography   83

Chapter 3: What Happens When Someone Needs Help Conceiving?

Chapter Preface   86

1. Too Often, Women Are Blamed When a Couple
   Has Trouble Conceiving   88
   Philip Teg-Nefaah Tabong and Philip Baba Adongo
2. Becoming a Parent Through Surrogacy Can Be a
   Positive Experience   94
   Danielle Tumminio Hansen
3. A Global Approach to Surrogacy Is Needed to Stop
   Exploitation of Women   101
   Herjeet Marway and Gulzaar Barn
4. Sperm Donation Must Be Regulated   105
   Naomi Cahn and Sonia Suter
5. Donors Are Not Entitled to Information About
   Children Conceived from Their Gametes   111
   Inez Raes, An Ravelingien, and Guido Pennings
6. Infertility Grief Continues with Decisions over
   Leftover Embryos   115
   Juli Fraga

Periodical and Internet Sources Bibliography   119

Chapter 4: What Reproductive Health Concerns Do Women Face?

Chapter Preface   122

1. LGBTQ People Need and Deserve Tailored Sexual
   and Reproductive Health Care   124
   Ruth Dawson and Tracy Leong
2. High Rates of Unintended Pregnancies Linked to
   Gaps in Family Planning Services   132
   World Health Organization
3. The Affordable Care Act Is Essential for the
   Reproductive Health of Women of Color   136
   Heidi Williamson
4. Stigma Hinders Treatment for Postpartum
   Depression   143
   Joanne Silberner
5. Pregnant Employees Must Not Be Seen as a Liability   148
   Rasheeda Bhagat
6. Period Leave Can Help Women in the Workforce   152
   Surekha Ragavan
7. Women Should Not Be Entitled to Menstrual Leave   159
   Radhika Santhanam

Periodical and Internet Sources Bibliography   166
For Further Discussion   167
Organizations to Contact   169
Bibliography of Books   172
Index   174

The Importance of Opposing Viewpoints

Perhaps every generation experiences a period in time in which the populace seems especially polarized, starkly divided on the important issues of the day and gravitating toward the far ends of the political spectrum and away from a consensus-facilitating middle ground. The world that today's students are growing up in and that they will soon enter into as active and engaged citizens is deeply fragmented in just this way. Issues relating to terrorism, immigration, women's rights, minority rights, race relations, health care, taxation, wealth and poverty, the environment, policing, military intervention, the proper role of government—in some ways, perennial issues that are freshly and uniquely urgent and vital with each new generation—are currently roiling the world.

If we are to foster a knowledgeable, responsible, active, and engaged citizenry among today's youth, we must provide them with the intellectual, interpretive, and critical-thinking tools and experience necessary to make sense of the world around them and of the all-important debates and arguments that inform it. After all, the outcome of these debates will in large measure determine the future course, prospects, and outcomes of the world and its peoples, particularly its youth. If they are to become successful members of society and productive and informed citizens, students need to learn how to evaluate the strengths and weaknesses of someone else's arguments, how to sift fact from opinion and fallacy, and how to test the relative merits and validity of their own opinions against the known facts and the best possible available information. The landmark series Opposing Viewpoints has been providing students with just such critical-thinking skills and exposure to the debates surrounding society's most urgent contemporary issues for many years, and it continues to serve this essential role with undiminished commitment, care, and rigor.

The key to the series's success in achieving its goal of sharpening students' critical-thinking and analytic skills resides in its title—

Opposing Viewpoints. In every intriguing, compelling, and engaging volume of this series, readers are presented with the widest possible spectrum of distinct viewpoints, expert opinions, and informed argumentation and commentary, supplied by some of today's leading academics, thinkers, analysts, politicians, policy makers, economists, activists, change agents, and advocates. Every opinion and argument anthologized here is presented objectively and accorded respect. There is no editorializing in any introductory text or in the arrangement and order of the pieces. No piece is included as a "straw man," an easy ideological target for cheap point-scoring. As wide and inclusive a range of viewpoints as possible is offered, with no privileging of one particular political ideology or cultural perspective over another. It is left to each individual reader to evaluate the relative merits of each argument—as he or she sees it, and with the use of ever-growing critical-thinking skills—and grapple with his or her own assumptions, beliefs, and perspectives to determine how convincing or successful any given argument is and how the reader's own stance on the issue may be modified or altered in response to it.

This process is facilitated and supported by volume, chapter, and selection introductions that provide readers with the essential context they need to begin engaging with the spotlighted issues, with the debates surrounding them, and with their own perhaps shifting or nascent opinions on them. In addition, guided reading and discussion questions encourage readers to determine the authors' point of view and purpose, interrogate and analyze the various arguments and their rhetoric and structure, evaluate the arguments' strengths and weaknesses, test their claims against available facts and evidence, judge the validity of the reasoning, and bring into clearer, sharper focus the reader's own beliefs and conclusions and how they may differ from or align with those in the collection or those of their classmates.

Research has shown that reading comprehension skills improve dramatically when students are provided with compelling, intriguing, and relevant "discussable" texts. The subject matter of these collections could not be more compelling, intriguing, or urgently relevant to today's students and the world they are poised to inherit. The anthologized articles and the reading and discussion questions that are included with them also provide the basis for stimulating, lively, and passionate classroom debates. Students who are compelled to anticipate objections to their own argument and identify the flaws in those of an opponent read more carefully, think more critically, and steep themselves in relevant context, facts, and information more thoroughly. In short, using discussable text of the kind provided by every single volume in the Opposing Viewpoints series encourages close reading, facilitates reading comprehension, fosters research, strengthens critical thinking, and greatly enlivens and energizes classroom discussion and participation. The entire learning process is deepened, extended, and strengthened.

For all of these reasons, Opposing Viewpoints continues to be exactly the right resource at exactly the right time—when we most need to provide readers with the critical-thinking tools and skills that will not only serve them well in school but also in their careers and their daily lives as decision-making family members, community members, and citizens. This series encourages respectful engagement with and analysis of opposing viewpoints and fosters a resulting increase in the strength and rigor of one's own opinions and stances. As such, it helps make readers "future ready," and that readiness will pay rich dividends for the readers themselves, for the citizenry, for our society, and for the world at large.

Introduction

> "...couples have a basic human right to decide freely and responsibly on the number and spacing of their children and a right to adequate education and information in this respect."
>
> — from the Resolution XVIII on the Human Rights Aspects of Family Planning adopted by the United Nations in the International Conference on Human Rights Tehran, Republic of Iran, April 22–May 13 1968[1]

Reproductive rights cover many aspects of human rights, including the right to sex education, access to safe abortion, and to family planning. They are widely contested rights, mostly because of how they conflict with religious and traditional beliefs. All things considered, reproductive rights address individual rights to have autonomy over their bodies, sexuality, sexual health, and reproductive choices.

The United Nations recognized reproductive rights as part of human rights in the Proclamation of Teheran, which was adopted on May 13, 1968.[2] This proclamation upheld the rights of parents to decide the planning of their family as seen in the quote above. Countries around the world have also adopted their own laws to protect families and reproductive health, but in many cases, they have become polarized, divisive laws.

Introduction

Abortion is illegal in many countries. In fact, the Center for Reproductive Rights explains that in 2019, there were 24 countries where abortion is completely prohibited, including Nicaragua, Egypt, and the Philippines.[3] In the United States, the landmark Supreme Court decision *Roe v. Wade* (1973) made the right to an abortion federal law, but abortion remained heavily challenged. On June 24, 2022, the Supreme Court struck down *Roe v. Wade*, undoing nearly 50 years of precedent. It is now up to each state to decide the fate of abortion rights. The United States is now gearing for a world post *Roe*. It may take years to fully understand what this means for reproductive rights.

Reproductive rights are constantly at odds with religious and conservative beliefs. For instance, sex education is a right protected by the United Nations. But many struggle with accepting it as a right, as they feel like sex should not be discussed in schools where teenagers and children learn. If it is addressed, many believe, it needs to primarily focus on abstinence. Nevertheless, critics argue that abstinence-only sex education hinders students' ability to fully grasp how to protect themselves and how to make the best decision about their reproductive health.

The question becomes: Is sex education a contested right because it is misunderstood, or does it indeed promote promiscuity? According to research conducted by Eva S. Goldfarb, Ph.D. and Lisa D. Lieberman, Ph.D., to be effective, comprehensive sex education should include discussion on "child abuse sex prevention, … sexual diversity, healthy relationships, dating and intimate partner violence," among others.[4] Moreover, consent is also a subject that many are pushing to be addressed. But should it be lumped into sex education discussions, or should it be addressed separately?

Many reproductive rights are crucial for women. Women often face discrimination in the workplace, and being a pregnant working woman has many challenges. The United States does not have a federal law for paid parental leave[5], which means maternity leave is offered at the discretion of a woman or nonbinary person's employer.

Studies have shown that paid parental leave "increases women's participation in the workforce and reduces gender pay gaps."[5] Whether it means that it should become a federal law remains to be seen. More questions need to be addressed as well, including: how long should maternity leave ideally be? Should fathers also be eligible for parental leave?

Those are only some of the issues covered by reproductive rights. *Opposing Viewpoints: Reproductive Rights* offers diverse perspectives written by a variety of authoritative voices in the field. In chapters titled "Should Abortions Be Legal?"; "Is Sex Education a Right?"; "What Happens When Someone Needs Help Conceiving?"; and "What Reproductive Health Concerns Do Women Face?", students will come away with a comprehensive understanding of some of the most contested issues confronted by women today.

Endnotes

1. Department of Economic and Social Affairs, "Reproductive rights," United Nations, n.d. https://www.un.org/en/development/desa/population/theme/rights/index.asp
2. "International conference on human rights," United Nations Population Fund, April 22, 1968. https://www.unfpa.org/events/international-conference-human-rights
3. "The world's abortion laws," Center for Reproductive Rights, n.d. https://reproductiverights.org/maps/worlds-abortion-laws/?category[1348]=1348
4. "The future of sex education," Futureofsexed.org, n.d. https://www.futureofsexed.org
5. Ellen Francis, Helier Cheung and Miriam Berger, "How does the U.S. compare to other countries on paid parental leave? Americans get 0 weeks. Estonians get more than 80." The Washington Post, November 11, 2021. https://www.washingtonpost.com/world/2021/11/11/global-paid-parental-leave-us/

CHAPTER 1

Should Abortions Be Legal?

Chapter Preface

Abortion is the most debated subset of reproductive rights. It is a practice that is illegal in many countries. Those who do not oppose abortion describe it as a health-care necessity for women. They believe it should be made available because even in countries where abortion is illegal, women and girls continue to seek it. By making abortions illegal, the argument goes, states increase the risk of injury and death in unsafe abortion practices. By providing safe abortion access, some experts believe that countries help curb the number of deaths by botched abortion.

In the argument supporting abortion access, there are also nuances. At what point during the pregnancy should abortion be permitted? What conditions should justify abortion? Experts have varying opinions. At the center of the debate is a divisive view of what a fetus is. Those who oppose abortions argue that life begins at conception. Therefore, when a fetus is removed from the womb, a human being is being killed. The fight against abortion is, according to them, a fight for life. Some anti-abortion advocates allow for termination of a pregnancy in the instance of rape and incest. Some are agreeable to abortion when the mother's life is in danger. However, many also believe that abortion should be illegal with no exception.

Those who support abortion believe that an embryo should not be considered a full human, offering their scientific take on when life actually begins. According to them, a woman should not be forced to carry a fetus to term if she doesn't want to.

In the United States, abortion was illegal until *Roe v. Wade*, which made abortion a constitutional right. But that ruling didn't mean that abortion stopped being a contested topic. Many laws in the United States started to find ways around *Roe v. Wade* to restrict access to abortions until *Roe* was officially struck down. The following chapter takes a closer look at the arguments for and against the right to choose, addressing questions varying from when life begins to who benefits from abortion.

VIEWPOINT 1

> *"When governments restrict access to abortions, people are compelled to resort to clandestine, unsafe abortions, particularly those who cannot afford to travel or seek private care."*

Criminalizing Abortion Only Makes Abortion Less Safe

Amnesty International

In the following viewpoint, Amnesty International argues that by criminalizing abortion, states are doing a disservice to women and girls. Even in countries where abortion is completely illegal, women still seek this procedure and are forced to turn to to unsafe measures. Abortion is a basic need, the author contends. Abortion is a safe medical procedure, and criminalizing it leads to preventable deaths and injury. The World Health Organization determines that 25 million unsafe abortions take place in a year. In addition, most of those cases take place in developing countries. By giving women access to not only safe abortion options but contraception and sex education, states can help prevent unnecessary deaths. Amnesty International is a nongovernmental organization that fights for human rights around the globe.

"Key Facts on Abortion," Amnesty International. Reprinted by permission.

As you read, consider the following questions:

1. What did the abortion rate in countries that prohibit abortion altogether and the abortion rate in countries that allow it only in instances to save a woman's life reveal about pregnacy termination?
2. What is one of the firsts steps that the WHO noted can help avoid maternal deaths and injury?
3. When did Ireland change its law to allow greater access to abortion?

An abortion is a medical procedure that ends a pregnancy. It is a basic healthcare need for millions of women, girls and others who can become pregnant. Worldwide, an estimated 1 in 4 pregnancies end in an abortion every year.

But while the need for abortion is common, access to safe and legal abortion services is far from guaranteed for those who may need abortion services.

In fact, access to abortion is one of the most hotly contested topics globally, and the debate is clouded by misinformation about the true ramifications of restricting access to this basic healthcare service.

Here are the basic facts about abortion that everyone should know.

People Have Abortions All the Time, Regardless of What the Law Says

Ending a pregnancy is a common decision that millions of people make—every year a quarter of pregnancies end in abortion.

And regardless of whether abortion is legal or not, people still require and regularly access abortion services. According to the Guttmacher Institute, a US-based reproductive health non-profit, the abortion rate is 37 per 1,000 people in countries that prohibit abortion altogether or allow it only in instances to save a woman's life, and 34 per 1,000 people in countries that broadly allow for abortion, a difference that is not statistically significant.

When undertaken by a trained health-care provider in sanitary conditions, abortions are one of the safest medical procedures available, safer even than child birth.

But when governments restrict access to abortions, people are compelled to resort to clandestine, unsafe abortions, particularly those who cannot afford to travel or seek private care. Which brings us to the next point.

Criminalising Abortion Does Not Stop Abortions, It Just Makes Abortion Less Safe

Preventing women and girls from accessing an abortion does not mean they stop needing one. That's why attempts to ban or restrict abortions do nothing to reduce the number of abortions, it only forces people to seek out unsafe abortions.

Unsafe abortions are defined by the World Health Organisation (WHO) as "a procedure for terminating an unintended pregnancy carried out either by persons lacking the necessary skills or in an environment that does not confirm to minimal medical standards, or both."

They estimate that 25 million unsafe abortions take place each year, the vast majority of them in developing countries.

In contrast to a legal abortion that is carried out by a trained medical provider, unsafe abortions can have fatal consequences. So much so that unsafe abortions are the third leading cause of maternal deaths worldwide and lead to an additional five million largely preventable disabilities, according to the WHO.

Almost Every Death and Injury from Unsafe Abortion Is Preventable

Deaths and injuries from unsafe abortions are preventable. Yet such deaths are common in countries where access to safe abortion is limited or prohibited entirely, as the majority of women and girls who need an abortion because of an unwanted pregnancy are not able to legally access one.

In countries with such restrictions, the law typically allows for what are known as narrow exceptions to the legislation criminalising abortion. These exceptions might be when pregnancy results from rape or incest, in cases of severe and fatal foetal impairment, or when there is risk to the life or health of the pregnant person. Only a small percentage of abortions are due to these reasons, meaning the majority of women and girls living under these laws might be forced to seek unsafe abortions and put their health and lives at risk.

Those who are already marginalised are disproportionately affected by such laws as they have no means to seek safe and legal services in another country or access private care. They include women and girls on low income, refugees and migrants, adolescents, lesbian, bisexual cisgender women and girls, transgender or gender non-conforming individuals, minority or Indigenous women.

The WHO has noted that one of the first steps toward avoiding maternal deaths and injuries is for states to ensure that people have access to sex education, are able to use effective contraception, have safe and legal abortion, and are given timely care for complications.

Evidence shows that abortion rates are higher in countries where there is limited access to contraception. Abortion rates are lower where people, including adolescents have information about and can access modern contraceptive methods and where comprehensive sexuality education is available and there is access to safe and legal abortion on broad grounds.

Many Countries Are Starting to Change Their Laws to Allow for Greater Access to Abortion

Over the last 25 years, more than 50 countries have changed their laws to allow for greater access to abortion, at times recognizing the vital role that access to safe abortion plays in protecting women's lives and health. Ireland joined that list on 25 May 2018 when, in a long-awaited referendum, its people voted overwhelmingly to repeal the near-total constitutional ban on abortion.

Despite the trend towards reforming laws to prevent deaths and injuries, some countries, including Nicaragua and El Salvador, maintain draconian and discriminatory laws that still ban abortion in virtually all circumstances. In fact, according to the WHO, across the globe 40% of women of childbearing age live in countries with highly restrictive abortion laws, or where abortion is legal, is neither available or accessible. In these states, abortion is banned or only permitted in highly restricted circumstances, or if legal, is not accessible due to multiple barriers to access in practice.

Even in states with broader access to legal abortion, pregnant individuals can still face multiple restrictions on and barriers to access to services such as cost, biased counselling, mandatory waiting periods. The WHO has issued technical guidance for states on the need to identify and remove such barriers.

Criminalising or Restricting Abortion Prevents Doctors from Providing Basic Care

Criminalisation and restrictive laws on abortion prevent healthcare providers from doing their job properly and from providing the best care options for their patients, in line with good medical practice and their professional ethical responsibilities.

Criminalisation of abortion results in a "chilling effect", whereby medical professionals may not understand the bounds of the law or may apply the restrictions in a narrower way than required by the law. This may be because of a number of reasons, including personal beliefs, stigma about abortion, negative stereotypes about women and girls, or the fear of criminal liability.

It also deters women and girls from seeking post-abortion care for complications due to unsafe abortion or other pregnancy related complications.

Claire Malone, a young woman from Ireland, who already had two children, shared her harrowing testimony with Amnesty

International Ireland of how her right to health was undermined by not being able to access an abortion due to the country's strict abortion laws.

Claire has a number of complex and life-threatening health conditions, including pulmonary atresia and pulmonary hypertension and had her lung removed in 2014. If women with pulmonary hypertension become pregnant, they are at high risk of becoming even more gravely ill or dying in pregnancy. Claire knows this, which is what led her to seek a termination, a request that was denied by her doctors because the law prevented them from doing so.

"My doctors said they couldn't offer a termination as my life wasn't at risk right now, and that was it. I know they are bound by the law. But I felt like if I waited until my health got so bad that I could die, then it would be too late by then anyway. And why is a risk to my health, as bad as it already was, not enough? How much do I have to go through before my doctors are allowed to treat me?"

It's Not Just Cisgender Women and Girls Who Need Abortions

It is not only cisgender women and girls (women and girls who were assigned female at birth) who may need access to abortion services, but also intersex people, transgender men and boys, and people with other gender identities who have the reproductive capacity to become pregnant.

One of the foremost barriers to abortion access for these individuals and groups is lack of access to healthcare. Additionally, for those who do have access to healthcare, they may face stigma and biased views in the provision of healthcare, as well as presumptions that they do not need access to contraception and abortion-related information and services. In some contexts, 28% transgender and gender non-conforming individuals report facing harassment in medical settings, and 19% report being refused medical care altogether due to their transgender status, with even higher numbers among communities of colour. This is due to many intertwining factors of poverty and race and related intersectional discrimination.

Sexual and reproductive rights advocates and LGBTI rights activists are campaigning for raising awareness on this and making abortion services available, accessible and inclusive for everybody who needs it without discrimination on any grounds.

Abortion Rights Must Be Respected

Ipas works for a world where sexual and reproductive rights are respected, protected and fulfilled. Reproductive rights, including abortion rights, are human rights. Everyone has the right to make informed decisions about their body and health—and to determine whether or when to bear children.

The right to an abortion is not a standalone right. It depends upon people also having other human rights: to health, to equality, to privacy and to live free from violence and discrimination. That's why Ipas works with diverse partners toward a world where all human rights—including sexual and reproductive rights—are respected, protected and fulfilled.

Restrictive abortion laws violate women's rights, including the right to life, to health, to equality, to privacy, and to live free from discrimination. We advocate within the United Nations' human rights bodies and other systems—at the global, regional and national levels—to advance abortion rights in international agreements, programs of action, and human rights jurisprudence. Our experts around the world are uniquely positioned to bring evidence and firsthand experience to present at international discussions about human rights and abortion.

At the national level in countries around the world, we work within partnerships and coalitions to hold governments accountable to their human rights obligations. For example, in Nicaragua, where abortion is banned entirely, we advocate with the Inter-American Commission on Human Rights to recommend that the government repeal the ban and uphold its citizens' rights.

"Human Rights and Abortion," Ipas.

Criminalising Abortion Is a Form of Discrimination, Which Further Fuels Stigma

Firstly, the denial of medical services, including reproductive health services that only certain individuals need is a form of discrimination.

The committee for the United Nations Convention on the Elimination of All Forms of Discrimination Against Women (CEDAW, or the Treaty for the Rights of Women), has consistently stated that restrictive abortion laws constitute discrimination against women. This applies to all women and people who can become pregnant, as the CEDAW Committee has confirmed that CEDAW's protections, and states' related obligations, apply to all women and therefore include discrimination against women who are lesbians, bisexual, and/or transgender, particularly given the specific forms of gendered discrimination they face.

Secondly, stigma around abortion and gender stereotyping is closely linked to the criminalisation of abortion and other restrictive abortion laws and policies.

The mere perception that abortion is unlawful or immoral leads to the stigmatization of women and girls by health care staff, family members, and the judiciary, among others. Consequently, women and girls seeking abortion risk discrimination and harassment. Some women have reported being abused and shamed by health care providers when seeking abortion services or post-abortion care.

Access to Safe Abortion Is a Matter of Human Rights

Access to safe abortion services is a human right. Under international human rights law, everyone has a right to life, a right to health, and a right to be free from violence, discrimination, and torture or cruel, inhuman and degrading treatment.

Human rights law clearly spells out that decisions about your body are yours alone—this is what is known as bodily autonomy.

Forcing someone to carry on an unwanted pregnancy, or forcing them to seek out an unsafe abortion, is a violation of their human rights, including the rights to privacy and bodily autonomy.

In many circumstances, those who have no choice but to resort to unsafe abortions also risk prosecution and punishment, including imprisonment, and can face cruel, inhuman and degrading treatment and discrimination in, and exclusion from, vital post-abortion health care.

Access to abortion is therefore fundamentally linked to protecting and upholding the human rights of women, girls and others who can become pregnant, and thus for achieving social and gender justice.

Amnesty International believes that everyone should be free to exercise their bodily autonomy and make their own decisions about their reproductive lives including when and if they have children. It is essential that laws relating to abortion respect, protect and fulfil the human rights of pregnant persons and not force them to seek out unsafe abortions.

VIEWPOINT 2

> *"The fetus's moral right to life simply does not include the right to use another person's body to stay alive."*

The U.S. Abortion Bans Abuse Women's Personal Freedom

Kimberley Brownlee

In the following viewpoint, Kimberley Brownlee quotes the philosopher Judith Jarvis Thomson to argue that it is beyond unjust to expect women and girls to carry a fetus for nine months if the pregnancy is unintended or unwanted, especially if it is the result of rape. Using their body to keep a fetus alive violates their rights. Thomson argues that abortion bans urge women to be Good Samaritans, but when we analyze the relevant verse from the Bible, we soon realize that the Good Samaritan is not forced to help the man in need beyond what he can offer. Note: The Dobbs case mentioned here was decided five months after this viewpoint was originally published. Kimberley Brownlee is a Canada Research Chair and Professor of Philosophy at the University of British Columbia.

"U.S. Abortion Bans Compel Women to Be Not Just Good Samaritans, but 'Splendid' Ones," by Kimberley Brownlee, The Conversation, January 4, 2022. https://theconversation.com/u-s-abortion-bans-compel-women-to-be-not-just-good-samaritans-but-splendid-ones-173220. Licensed under CC BY-4.0 International.

As you read, consider the following questions:

1. When did the Supreme Court hear the oral arguments in the *Dobbs vs. Jackson Women's Health Organization* case?
2. According to the U.S. Centers for Disease Control and Prevention, how many women endure rape-related pregnancy?
3. The Texas law permits abortions, but only in "medical emergencies." What are some questions/concerns highlighted by the author in this viewpoint?

If a music lovers' society kidnaps you and attaches you at the kidneys to a famous violinist with a fatal disease, are you required to stay and keep him alive for nine months until he recovers?

This is the well-known thought experiment posed by the late American philosopher Judith Jarvis Thomson in "A Defense of Abortion." The essay was published prior to Roe vs. Wade, the 1973 United States Supreme Court ruling that held that the U.S. Constitution protects a woman's right to abortion without excessive government restriction.

Thomson argued that, although it would be nice of you to stay attached to the violinist until he gets better, no one could force you to. The violinist is, of course, a person with full moral status. He simply doesn't have a right—innocent or not—to use your body to keep himself alive.

Thomson said pregnancy is similar.

When Does Personhood Begin?

The year ahead is an important one for abortion rights in the United States. In December 2021, the U.S. Supreme Court heard oral arguments in *Dobbs vs. Jackson Women's Health Organization*, a case involving Mississippi's ban of nearly all abortions after 15 weeks. The court will rule on the ban in June.

Supreme Court justices asked Mississippi Solicitor General Scott Stewart whether any secular philosophers and bioethicists think the rights of personhood begin at conception or before viability.

Thomson certainly didn't think fetuses are people any more than acorns are oak trees. But, crucially, she said we could assume that fetuses have all the rights of personhood and still defend abortion. The fetus's moral right to life simply does not include the right to use another person's body to stay alive.

Many commentators have tried to poke holes in Thomson's thought experiment, searching for light between the famous violinist and pregnancy.

Some commentators stress that the violinist is a stranger but the fetus is "hers." But not every woman carries a fetus that is genetically hers. And only a few people would condemn the violinist's brother if he refused to stay put for nine months.

Some commentators argue that women aren't kidnapped into pregnancy like the person in the thought experiment is. But rape is all too common. A study cited by the U.S. Centers for Disease Control and Prevention reports that about three million American women endure rape-related pregnancy and 18 million endure vaginal rape during their lifetime. The new Texas heartbeat law banning abortion after six weeks makes no exception for rape or incest.

Other commentators argue that women and girls who aren't raped know that if they have sex with men, they risk becoming pregnant.

This ignores that many girls—especially those raised in conservative religious communities—don't know how pregnancy occurs. Democratic California congresswoman Barbara Lee, who testified at a congressional hearing on reproductive rights last year, said that sex education was non-existent in her Catholic school, and she was unsure how girls became pregnant until she discovered at 16 that she was.

The Good Samaritan Argument

The rest of Thomson's defence of abortion is less well-known, but key to the current debate.

Thomson argued that requiring women to carry unwanted pregnancies to term compels them to be Good Samaritans. This is a radical understatement.

In the well-known biblical parable Luke 10:25-37, a priest and a Levite cross the road to get away from a man who'd been attacked and left for dead while journeying to Jericho. The Good Samaritan takes pity on the man, bandages his wounds and takes him on his donkey to an inn to care for him. The next day, the Good Samaritan gives the innkeeper money and says: "Look after him and when I return, I will reimburse you for any extra expense you may have."

Notice that the Good Samaritan isn't forced to step up, and after he takes the man to an inn, he outsources the rest of the job. It's the innkeeper—not the Good Samaritan—who nurses the man, and he does it for a price.

Finally, the Good Samaritan faces no personal risk to his health, life or livelihood. And once he has done his good deed, he can carry on his way with no lasting remorse about whether he really should have cared for the man for the next 18 years instead of handing him over to others.

If the U.S. Supreme Court overturns abortion rights, American women and girls will be compelled to be not just Good Samaritans in carrying unwanted pregnancies to term, but what Thomson calls Splendid Samaritans who are required to risk their lives, health and security to help someone in need.

The Texas law permits abortions, but only in "medical emergencies," which are left undefined. As the New York Times asks: Does cancer count, or a heart condition that could lead to sudden cardiac arrest?

Good Samaritan Laws

The real kicker is that what was true in Thomson's America of the 1970s is true now. Except in a few states that have duties to aid in limited circumstances, no American is legally required to help others in need, even when they can do so easily.

Good Samaritan laws exist in many countries and require people to help their fellow citizens in need whenever they can, or risk penalty. But in the U.S., no one is compelled to be even a Minimally Decent Samaritan. There is no duty to give blood. No duty to be an organ donor. No duty to put yourself out generally to help others in need.

Thomson observed that those pushing for abortion restrictions "had better start working for the adoption of Good Samaritan laws generally, or earn the charge that they are acting in bad faith."

Yet for better or worse, legal duties to aid are antithetical to the negatively framed U.S. Constitution that stresses individual liberties but offers few positive provisions.

Thomson's defence of abortion isn't unqualified. She said that if pregnancy came with no risks, took only an hour and left no lasting residue, then a person would be morally callous, self-centred and indecent not to carry a pregnancy to term. However, that person still has a right to do the indecent thing. This is what liberty rights do: they protect us in acting in ways others find objectionable.

How many other spaces for personal freedom would logically collapse if the U.S. Supreme Court stamps out this one in June?

VIEWPOINT 3

> "Abortion...is a rejection of equal human dignity, not an affirmation of it, because it takes the life of an innocent human person."

Abortion Is Not the Answer to Gender Inequality

Paul Stark

In the following viewpoint, Paul Stark agrees that women and mothers do tend to carry a disproportionate amount of the responsibility when it comes to pregnancy and childcare. However, he does not believe that this is enough of a reason to deny a fetus the chance to live. As his argument goes, we have an obligation toward the unborn child. The right course of action should be adoption. In addition, men should also be held accountable and should be prevented from shunning their responsibilities. Abortion will not solve the gender equality issue, as the fight against abortion is not gender centric. Paul Stark is Communications Director of Minnesota Citizens Concerned for Life.

As you read, consider the following questions:

1. What are the author's four arguments against grounding a constitutional right to abortion in the Equal Protection Clause of the Fourteenth Amendment?

"The Gender Equality Argument for Abortion," by Paul Stark, MCCL, March 14, 2017. Reprinted by permission.

2. Why does the author believe that women don't need abortions to achieve social equality?
3. Who wrote the essay "Abortion as a Feminist Concern"?

Some people argue that gender equality requires legalized abortion. After all, the challenges of pregnancy and childbirth fall on women but not on men. Only with access to abortion, then, can women be truly equal and free to determine the course of their lives.

"Pregnancy and childbirth ... serve to restrict women's ability to participate in society on equal footing with men," writes feminist author Katha Pollitt. "[W]e must ... ensure that our daughters have the same rights, freedoms, and opportunities as our sons to fulfill their dreams," says former President Barack Obama.

Some legal scholars, including U.S. Supreme Court Justice Ruth Bader Ginsburg, aim to ground a constitutional right to abortion in the Equal Protection Clause of the Fourteenth Amendment ("no state shall ... deny to any person within its jurisdiction the equal protection of the laws") rather than in the Due Process Clause (as the Court did in *Roe v. Wade*). Equality under the law, they say, requires abortion access.

This argument does not withstand scrutiny. First, unequal burdens don't justify the killing of innocent human beings. The burdens of caring for five-year-old children, for example, fall disproportionately on the parents of five-year-old children. Laws against killing or abandoning five-year-olds do not affect everyone in the same way—one might even claim that they deprive parents of "the same rights, freedoms, and opportunities" as non-parents. But clearly they are not wrong.

Likewise, the challenges of pregnancy fall on women and not men, and a law against killing unborn children by abortion would impact women in a way that it does not impact men. But such a law would not be unjust for that reason. Laws may *affect* people differently given different circumstances, but that does not mean that they *treat* people differently. Everyone should be equally prohibited from killing innocent human beings. This prohibition is not gender-specific.

Second, men and women are equally morally responsible for their offspring, even though this obligation can take different forms (women, by virtue of reproductive biology, uniquely gestate children). Men can more easily run from their parental duties than women, but the solution to this dereliction is not to authorize the killing of human beings before they are born (which is a further dereliction). Rather, men must accept responsibility and be held responsible by law when necessary.

Third, the argument from gender equality seems to presuppose that pregnancy is a disability and that pregnant women need surgery (abortion) to become equal to men. This view effectively disparages women and their reproductive powers while elevating men to the paradigm of human sexuality.

"Sexual equality via abortion looks to cure biological asymmetry—the fact that women get pregnant and men don't—by promoting the rejection of women's bodies," writes feminist scholar Erika Bachiochi. "Authentic equality and reproductive justice would demand something far more revolutionary: that men and society at large respect and support women in their myriad capacities and talents which include, for most women at some time in their lives, childbearing."

Fourth, women don't need abortion to achieve social equality, professional success, and personal fulfillment. "Why is it that we assume women are incapable of dealing with the adversity of an unwanted pregnancy by any other means than that of destroying life? Is this a flattering view of women?" asked moral philosopher Janet E. Smith in her 1978 essay "Abortion as a Feminist Concern."

Of course, mothers often experience enormous and unfair difficulties. Placing a child for adoption, though, is an ethical and life-affirming way to relinquish responsibility, and pregnancy care centers, government programs, and other forms of assistance enable women in need to meet the challenges of pregnancy and parenthood. But more can and should be done to accommodate the essential role mothers play in our society.

Abortion, however, is a rejection of equal human dignity, not an affirmation of it, because it takes the life of an innocent human person. Legalized abortion excludes an entire class of human beings from the protection of the law by allowing them to be dismembered and killed at the discretion of others. "Women will never climb to equality and social empowerment over mounds of dead fetuses," quips Hastings Center scholar and feminist writer Sidney Callahan.

There is no equality in abortion.

VIEWPOINT 4

> "First and foremost, men's 'right to an abortion' is predicated on the idea that children—and fetuses—are pieces of property jointly owned by men and women..."

Men Should Not Have Abortion Rights

Marcus Lee

What about men's rights? That is one of the criticisms of granting women the right to abort a fetus. In this viewpoint, Marcus Lee explains that men are not entitled to abortion rights. Arguing that men should be taken into consideration when talking about abortion rights proves the bigotry leading the men's rights movement, he argues. It is deeply rooted in a racist and sexist ethos that we should have moved away from. Bodies are not properties, and believing that men are entitled to have a say in decisions about women's bodies is profoundly wrong and inaccurate. At the time of this viewpoint's original publication, Marcus Lee was a student at Morehouse College.

As you read, consider the following questions:

1. What does MRAs stand for, and what do they fight for?
2. Who sponsored HB 252?
3. Why does the author believe the logic of the MRAs fail?

"Sorry, Men's Rights Activists, You Don't Have Abortion 'Rights,'" by Marcus Lee, Rewire News Group, March 11, 2014. Reprinted by permission.

Central to the political agenda of men's rights activists is floating the idea that men somehow have a "right" to an abortion, or more accurately a right to interfere with a woman's right to an abortion—an argument that highlights the intersecting bigotries embedded in the men's rights movement.

Some of the most dangerous anti-woman work is done at the hands of so-called men's rights activists (MRAs). Initially organizing themselves in the '70s as a response to what they claimed was the rise of "misandry," MRAs push for a more patriarchal society—one that's organized by "natural" gender roles and supposedly gender-blind but actually male-dominated state governance. For example, A Voice for Men, an online men's rights organization founded in 2009, has as the first goal of its mission statement the exposure of "misandry and gender-centrism on all levels in our culture." Here, the group immediately associates gendered analyses of society with the hatred of men, hence promoting disregard for and ignorance of the suppression of women.

Central to the political agenda of MRAs is floating the idea that men somehow have a "right" to an abortion, or more accurately a right to interfere with a woman's right to an abortion. MRAs argue that women's autonomy is directly oppressive to men because men are disallowed input as to whether or not women should give birth. Thus, they argue that the state should intervene by forcing women to consult men before they can legally abort a pregnancy or that women or doctors should be held legally accountable to men after an abortion has taken place, usurping their right to self-determine.

Unfortunately, this hazardous ideology has been taken seriously and supported by a few lawmakers. For example, in 2009 Ohio state Rep. John Adams (R-Sidney) sponsored HB 252, which would have assigned men direct control over women's bodies by requiring doctors to receive written consent from the father of the fetus before a woman could have an abortion. Similarly, under an anti-racist, anti-sexist guise, Rep. Trent Franks (R-AZ) sponsored HR 447 in this current session of Congress to "prohibit discrimination against the unborn on the basis of sex or race, and for other purposes." Here, Franks attempts, ironically, to imagine a reputable justification for control over women's bodies by questioning their motivations for an abortion and by situating himself, doctors, and men in general as social justice deputies.

Given that these efforts are seeping into multiple state and federal legislatures, the rhetoric and strategies employed by MRAs must be taken seriously. They are deeply problematic and counterproductive to women's liberation and gender equity. However, they also pose problems to racial equity and sexual freedom. Through a specific examination of MRAs pushing for their own set of "abortion rights," it is possible to highlight the intersecting bigotries embedded in the men's rights movement.

Acknowledging how oppressions rely on one another helps to deconstruct them. Looking through this intersectional lens reveals that the argument for an alleged men's right to an abortion relies on racist conceptions of bodies as property, and heterosexist, traditionalist ideas about female eroticism. It is important to note that the men's rights push for abortion rights is representative, not exemplary—that is, "men's abortion rights" initiatives should be understood simply as puzzle pieces within the larger, problematic universe of the men's rights movement.

First and foremost, men's "right to an abortion" is predicated on the idea that children—and fetuses—are pieces of property jointly owned by men and women; their arguments insinuate that if children are property, then it follows that it is unfair for a woman to have complete control over whether or not a potential piece of property over which she shares ownership with a man materializes. This conception of children is evident in MRA-influenced legislation. For example, Franks' HR 447, the "Prenatal Nondiscrimination Act" (PRENDA), would authorize civil actions for verifiable money damages for injuries and punitive damages by fathers and maternal grandmothers. In this way of thinking, children, unborn fetuses, and women's uteruses become properties that can be assigned a dollar amount by men who moreover exert ownership. Because the fetus and the uterus are inextricable, women are necessarily implicated by the conception of children and the fetus as property.

Additionally, conceiving of children as property is a direct strike against the fight for racial equity as it comes out of an anti-Black ethos. The abolition of slavery should have been accompanied by the total deracination of each constituent part of its ethos. In other words, if we think of slavery as a poisonous cake, we shouldn't have just thrown out the cake; we should have thrown out each ingredient that led to the creation of the cake with the understanding that each intentionally added to the poison. Any time any of these ingredients are used in another recipe, the end product is dangerous. One of the main ingredients of slavery is the idea of people as property—Black bodies were things to be bought and sold among people who believed that they had ownership over them. In order to avoid reproducing any facet of the catastrophe that was slavery, the idea that people are property must be wholly eradicated for any and everybody.

Meanwhile, MRAs reproduce the ideology of slavery with their conception of children as property; consequently, working to reproduce an environment that is conducive to Black marginality and suffering. Thus, MRAs push for the right to an abortion is a significant obstruction to the struggle for gender and racial equity.

Furthermore, men's "right" to an abortion is predicated on an assumed traditional, male-centered sexuality where sex is defined by vaginal penetration, consent is simplified to yes or no, and women are subjected to expectations of compulsory availability and heterosexuality. Under this view, MRAs suggest that men are powerless with regard to impregnating women, and therefore need state intervention in order to remedy power imbalances.

In reality, understandings of sexuality should be complicated through a queer paradigm in order to make for an environment that is conducive to greater sexual freedom for women and men. Vaginal penetration is not the only form of sexuality to be performed.

Consent cannot be simplified to a yes or no—it is an ongoing negotiation of sexual practices, likes and dislikes, and desires and distastes. Sex may include the desire or the lack thereof to have a child, and the necessary precautions should be taken to make both parties comfortable with the encounter and its potential outcomes, including but not limited to condoms, spermicide, and non-penetrative sex. When consent is simplified to a yes or no, the vulnerability and comfort level of the passive partner during the encounter are disregarded.

Lastly, women cannot and should not be understood through a lens of compulsory availability and heterosexuality—women are indeed diverse people with different sexual desires, different life goals, and different attractions. They cannot be reduced to targets of male (hetero)sexual desire. When they are, queer people are unfairly placed on the periphery and non-queer people are the targets of uncomfortable encounters.

As they are used by MRAs in arguing for men's "right" to abortion and beyond, these assumptions together absolve men of all responsibility from necessary negotiation regarding sexual practices. This not only works to disenfranchise women, but also obstructs sexual freedom for women and men.

Finally, the logic of MRAs simply fails. They seem to employ a biological deterministic logic, arguing that if both men and women contribute to the biology of the fetus, then both should help determine what will happen to it. However, suddenly this biological deterministic logic is abandoned when examining female biology: Using the same lens, if the choice to have or not to have a child significantly affects the biology of a woman, then she should be able to make that decision for herself. MRAs conveniently adopt biological determinism, and then disregard it when it no longer works for them, consequently undermining their own argument.

In the end, the logic behind sexism always falls apart.

MRAs depend on sexism, racism, and heterosexism to work toward men's "right" to abortion and beyond. Relying on ideas of human bodies as property and female sexuality as necessarily traditional, heterosexual, and available, they create a severely dangerous logic aimed toward men exerting even greater control over women's bodies. If this analysis isn't convincing enough, one would need to only look toward the blog posts on the A Voice for Men website—one of which romanticizes racial terror by arguing that "misogynist" is the "new n-word." Highlighting these intersections is important, because doing so heightens the potential for intra-community coalition building within social justice movements.

VIEWPOINT 5

> "If Roe v Wade is overturned, abortion will still be safely and legally accessible for those who can afford it. The devastating consequences of such a decision will fall primarily on the shoulders of those least able to bear it."

When Abortion Is Illegal, Marginalized and Low-Income People Suffer the Most

Prudence Flowers

In 1973, the Supreme Court made abortion a constitutional right in Roe v Wade. *This decision has been challenged since its inception, but by the time Donald Trump was elected to the presidency in 2016, anti-abortion lawmakers were very close to pushing the Supreme Court to reverse* Roe. *Among the state laws passed to challenge* Roe *was a Mississippi law banning abortion after 15 weeks. Ultimately, it was the case challenging this law,* Dobbs v Jackson Women's Health Organization, *that compelled the Supreme Court to overturn* Roe. *In the following viewpoint, written before the decision, Prudence Flowers argues that it poses the most significant threat to* Roe v Wade *because of how it pushes boundaries and also because of the political leanings of the current Supreme Court. Prudence Flowers is Senior Lecturer in US History at Flinders University in Australia.*

"Will Roe v Wade Be Overturned, and What Would This Mean? The US Abortion Debate Explained," by Prudence Flowers, The Conversation, December 7, 2021. https://theconversation.com/will-roe-v-wade-be-overturned-and-what-would-this-mean-the-us-abortion-debate-explained-173156. Licensed under CC BY-4.0 International.

Reproductive Rights

As you read, consider the following questions:
1. Why is *Roe v Wade* sometimes described as a "super precedent?"
2. How many justices did President Donald Trump appoint to the Supreme Court?
3. How many states have laws that could be used to ban or severely restrict abortion?

Last week, the US Supreme Court heard oral arguments in a case that is the most significant threat to abortion rights in the US in decades.

The case, *Dobbs v Jackson Women's Health Organization*, centres on a 2018 Mississippi law banning abortion after 15 weeks except in "medical emergencies or for severe fetal abnormality".

It is part of a wave of state abortion bans passed since the 2016 US presidential election that take aim at *Roe v Wade*, the landmark 1973 Supreme Court decision that guaranteed abortion as a constitutional right.

So, what is this Mississippi challenge based on and could it eventually lead to the overturning of *Roe v Wade*?

Two Issues at Stake in the Mississippi Case

The Supreme Court, which likely won't make a decision in the case until mid-2022, is faced with two key issues.

One of the central elements of *Roe* is that the state and federal governments cannot ban abortion before viability, the point at which a fetus can theoretically survive outside the pregnant person's body (defined as approximately 23-24 weeks gestation).

The Mississippi ban falls well short of the viability threshold. As such, the Supreme Court is now considering whether all pre-viability bans on elective abortions are unconstitutional.

The second issue is respect for legal precedent. Since the Supreme Court was established in 1789, it has reversed its own constitutional precedents only 145 times, or in 0.5% of cases.

Roe v Wade, decided 48 years ago, is sometimes described as a "super precedent" decision, because the Supreme Court has repeatedly reaffirmed it.

Constitutional scholar Michael Gerhardt defines "super precedents" as

> constitutional decisions in which public institutions have heavily invested, repeatedly relied, and consistently supported over a significant period of time.

Conservatives, including several on the Supreme Court, reject the inclusion of *Roe v Wade* in this definition.

Why Does the Court's Makeup Now Matter?

In oral arguments, Mississippi's lawyers invited the Supreme Court to use this case to overturn *Roe v Wade*. Anti-abortion lawyers and activists are optimistic their arguments will fall on receptive ears.

In 2016, Donald Trump, like every Republican presidential candidate dating back to Ronald Reagan, campaigned on a promise to appoint "pro-life judges" to the Supreme Court.

Despite serving only one term in office, Trump was able to deliver. He appointed Neil Gorsuch in 2017, Brett Kavanaugh in 2018, and Amy Coney Barrett in 2020 to fill Supreme Court vacancies. Conservatives on the bench now have a 6-3 majority.

While conservative Chief Justice John Roberts is no supporter of abortion rights, he has been a swing vote on a range of issues and has an established interest in protecting the reputation of the Supreme Court. However, after Barrett was sworn in, conservatives no longer needed to appeal to him to form a majority.

And while Kavanaugh claimed in his confirmation hearings to believe *Roe v Wade* was "settled as a precedent of the Supreme Court", last week in oral arguments he read from a list of Supreme Court cases that overturned precedent.

How States Have Chipped Away at Abortion Access

Abortion rights have survived serious attacks before.

In *Planned Parenthood v Casey* (1992), three appointees of Republican presidents sided with two liberal justices to uphold *Roe v Wade*, arguing "liberty finds no refuge in a jurisprudence of doubt."

That judgment reiterated the viability threshold for legal abortions, but allowed states to pass restrictions as long as they did not place an "undue burden" on the right to an abortion.

Since the 1990s, anti-abortion lawmakers have pushed to find the limits of an "undue burden," pursuing laws and test cases that erode abortion access.

Many states now mandate 24- or 72-hour waiting periods, ultrasounds, parental consent requirements for teenagers and counselling that repeats anti-abortion claims.

Since 2010, conservative states have also passed hundreds of targeted regulation of abortion provision (TRAP) laws, which place prohibitive and medically unnecessary restrictions on doctors and clinics that provide abortion care.

This anti-abortion strategy of chipping away at *Roe v Wade* has been extraordinarily successful.

Between 2011–16, over 160 abortion providers closed or stopped offering terminations, the largest rate of closures since 1973. Multiple states, including Mississippi, have one remaining abortion clinic in operation.

New Strategy: More Aggressive Challenges to *Roe v Wade*

After Trump's victory, opponents of abortion shifted to a more aggressive strategy of directly challenging *Roe v Wade*.

Most of these recent laws, such as Alabama's 2019 near-total abortion ban, have been blocked by the lower courts.

A new Texas law banning abortion after six weeks is currently in effect while the Supreme Court considers whether its unique enforcement mechanism, which allows private citizens to sue anyone they think has broken the law, can be challenged in the courts.

And the partisan makeup of the current Supreme Court makes it almost certain that Mississippi's law will stand.

What is not clear is whether the justices will restrict themselves to the question of fetal viability or whether they will completely overturn *Roe v Wade*, allowing states to ban abortion at will.

If the Supreme Court allows the states to ban abortion before viability, this will have a significant impact on the small number of pregnant people who seek abortions in the second trimester.

Generally, these people have either received a devastating medical diagnosis or they have complex personal circumstances, including domestic violence, mental illness, and/or drug addiction. These patients, as well as the doctors that provide this care, are highly stigmatised.

The Long-Term Effects of Overturning Roe v Wade

If *Roe v Wade* is overturned and abortion rights are returned to the states, access to abortion will effectively be a geographical lottery.

Twenty-two states have laws that could be used to ban or severely restrict abortion, while 15 states and the District of Columbia have laws that protect the right to abortion.

Abortion is a routine, common type of reproductive health care. Approximately one in four American women will have an abortion before they are 45.

Despite the political controversy and polarising rhetoric, polling this year indicated that 80% of Americans support abortion in all or most cases, and at least 60% support *Roe v Wade*.

However, while abortion is common, three-quarters of US abortion patients are low income and more than half are people of colour. They already face significant financial and logistical barriers in accessing this essential health care.

If *Roe v Wade* is overturned, abortion will still be safely and legally accessible for those who can afford it. The devastating consequences of such a decision will fall primarily on the shoulders of those least able to bear it.

VIEWPOINT 6

> "It's so interesting that this idea that abortion hurts women has gone so far with no data, and that the idea that being denied an abortion hurts women has not yet carried in the same way."

Overturning *Roe* Is Out of Step with Public Opinion

Julie Rovner

In the following viewpoint, Julie Rovner writes about the inevitability of the end of Roe v. Wade *as the law of the land. The author argues that anti-abortion activists worked slowly and methodically to gain support on the issue, with the eventual goal being changes to legislation that allowed abortion. But public opinion on the issue has not changed much over the years, and still Roe is on the brink of being overturned. What happens when legislators are not in agreement with their constituents? They may eventually be voted out of office, but that will be little comfort to those seeking abortion procedures. Julie Rovner is chief Washington correspondent for Kaiser Health News.*

As you read, consider the following questions:

1. What was George W. Bush's advice to the anti-abortion faction of the Republican party?

"Fast-Tracked Ruling on Abortion Won't Wait for 'Hearts and Minds' to Change", by Julie Rovner, Kaiser Health News, 01/21/2022. https://khn.org/news/article/abortion-ruling-supreme-court-public-opinion/. Licensed under CC BY 4.0 International.

2. What is so extraordinary about the Texas law mentioned in the viewpoint?
3. What demographic is impacted the most by denied access to abortion?

When he was running for president in 1999, George W. Bush, then governor of Texas, famously fended off the strong anti-abortion wing of his party by suggesting the country ought not consider banning abortion until public opinion shifted further in that direction. "Laws are changed as minds are persuaded," he said.

Bush was no moderate on the abortion issue. As president he signed several pieces of anti-abortion legislation, including the first federal ban on a specific abortion procedure, and used his authority to severely limit federally funded research on embryonic stem cells.

But he was clear in urging anti-abortion allies to concentrate on persuading more Americans to take their side before pushing for broader restrictions. "I know as you return to your communities you will redouble your efforts to change hearts and minds, one person at a time," he told anti-abortion demonstrators at the annual March for Life rally in 2004. "This is the way we will build a lasting culture of life, a compassionate society in which every child is born into a loving family and protected by law." For many years after that, anti-abortion forces concentrated on more incremental steps, such as putting burdensome health and safety requirements on abortion clinics and requiring waiting periods before abortions.

It seems that strategy is about to be tested. Although public opinion on abortion has budged little in the ensuing two decades and the nation is still bitterly divided, the Supreme Court appears poised to overturn or at least significantly weaken its landmark abortion ruling, *Roe v. Wade*, decided 49 years ago this week.

Sometime in the coming weeks or months, justices will decide in a case from Mississippi whether bans on abortion before fetal viability can be constitutional. During those arguments in December, most of the justices in the court's new conservative majority seemed to question the constitutional foundation of the nearly 50-year-old precedent that guarantees the right to abortion nationwide. If a majority answers yes to allowing Mississippi's ban at 15 weeks of pregnancy, "that undoes *Roe*," said Marjorie Dannenfelser, who, as president of the Susan B. Anthony List, has been working toward that goal since the organization's 1992 founding.

Abortion-rights supporters also expect *Roe* to be overturned. In Texas, all but abortions performed in a pregnancy's earliest stages have been unavailable since September because of a legal standoff over a state law that bans abortions after six weeks but leaves enforcement to the general public, by authorizing civil suits against anyone who performs an abortion or "aids and abets" one.

"*Roe* has no meaning," Dr. Bhavik Kumar, a San Antonio abortion physician, told reporters on a conference call Jan. 18. "We're living in a place where abortion is essentially banned." Kumar said the Texas law, which the Supreme Court refused to block last month, means abortion is illegal "as soon as 10 days after a missed period for some women."

Dannenfelser said that even if the justices roll back *Roe*, groups like hers still want Americans to come to a consensus on the abortion issue, but it may not be a national agreement. "But that's what consensus is, it's the consensus of people living in [each] state," she said. "So it will be different in Alabama than in North Carolina, which will be different from the state of Washington, from Texas." And what if lawmakers turn out to be more anti-abortion than the people who elected them? "They get unelected," she said, but she also envisions the question working the other way. "And if they're not strong enough in their convictions on life, they'll be unelected."

Abortion-rights supporters say the public discussion has too long been marked by a lack of transparency. "We've had a decade-long campaign of misinformation and disinformation," said Kumar. "When people understand reality, when they understand science," he said, "it has a profound difference on their opinion."

That's where the Turnaway Study comes in. It's a 10-year look at nearly 1,000 women at 30 abortion clinics who got abortions or were "turned away" because they were too far along in their pregnancies. "We were interested in answering the question 'Does abortion hurt women?'" said Diana Greene Foster, the study's lead researcher and author of the book "The Turnaway Study: Ten Years, a Thousand Women, and the Consequences of Having—Or Being Denied—An Abortion." Abortion foes for years have claimed that abortion harms women's mental health and causes physical problems as well.

Data from the Turnaway Study has resulted in the publication of more than 50 peer-reviewed studies, and the answer to nearly all the questions asked, said Foster, is that the women who got abortions fared better in respect to economics and health, including their mental health, compared with those who did not have abortions.

"We see large immediate differences in the economic well-being where women who were denied abortions are more likely to be poor, less likely to be employed, more likely to say they don't have enough money for basic living needs," she said.

Yet that's not what much of the public hears. "It's so interesting that this idea that abortion hurts women has gone so far with no data, and that the idea that being denied an abortion hurts women has not yet carried in the same way," Foster said.

And in the end, public opinion really shouldn't even matter that much, said Dr. Jamila Perritt, an OB-GYN and abortion provider in Washington, D.C., and president and CEO of the abortion-rights advocacy group Physicians for Reproductive Health. "When you need access" to abortion care, she said, "the opinion of other people, who know nothing about your life, means little."

But it may help determine whether—and where—legal abortion remains available.

Reproductive Rights

Periodical and Internet Sources Bibliography

The following articles have been selected to supplement the diverse views presented in this chapter.

BBC, Ethics guide, "Moral personhood," BBC, n.d. https://www.bbc.co.uk/ethics/abortion/philosophical/moralperson.shtml

Megan Brenan, "Record-high 47% in U.S. think abortion is morally acceptable," Gallup, June 9, 2021. https://news.gallup.com/poll/350756/record-high-think-abortion-morally-acceptable.aspx

Center for Health Ethics, "Abortion," University of Missouri, School of Medicine, n.d. https://medicine.missouri.edu/centers-institutes-labs/health-ethics/faq/abortion

Rachel Elbaum and Nigel Chiwaya, "Abortion laws worldwide: In what countries is abortion legal?" NBC News, May 6, 2022. https://www.nbcnews.com/news/world/countries-abortion-legal-illegal-laws-rcna27505

Marquise Francis, "How abortion rights were won—and may soon be lost again," Yahoo! News, May 6, 2022. https://news.yahoo.com/how-abortion-rights-were-won-and-may-soon-be-lost-again-194335001.html

Joe Hernandez, "What overturning *Roe v. Wade* could mean for the rest of the world," NPR, May 5, 2022. https://www.npr.org/2022/05/05/1096738094/roe-v-wade-abortion-overturn-impact-world

Tim Johnson, "If you're really pro-life, read this." The Palm Beach Post, April 20, 2022. https://www.palmbeachpost.com/story/opinion/2022/04/20/minister-doctor-and-medical-editor-weighs-abortion-rights/7359036001/

Jerry Newcombe, "Abortion: Why this issue won't die," The Christian Post, January 23, 2021. https://www.christianpost.com/voices/abortion-why-this-issue-wont-die.html

Pew Research Center, "America's abortion quandary," May 6, 2022. https://www.pewresearch.org/religion/2022/05/06/americas-abortion-quandary/

Deborah Yetter, "Judge puts temporary hold on Kentucky abortion law, clearing way for services to resume," Courier Journal, April 21, 2022. https://www.courier-journal.com/story/news/politics/ky-general-assembly/2022/04/21/judge-temporarily-blocks-2022-kentucky-abortion-law/7318975001/

OPPOSING VIEWPOINTS® SERIES

CHAPTER 2

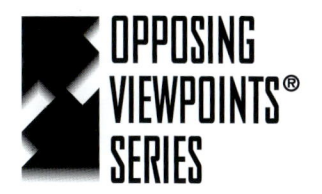

Is Sex Education a Right?

Chapter Preface

Even though many schools in the United States promote sex education, it is not always supported by parents and people with conservative views. When it is supported, opinions on how to approach it differ. Many believe that, for sex education to be effective, one must take a comprehensive approach to it, where contraceptive options, sexually transmitted diseases and infections, and consent are discussed. Teenagers are being bombarded with a barrage of inappropriate materials everywhere they go—from the media, online, and their peers. According to those who favor comprehensive sex education, giving students a complete sex and relationship education prepares them to make better decisions about their reproductive life.

Abstinence-only sex education focuses heavily on promoting abstinence among teens. The fear of those who oppose comprehensive sex education is that it endorses or encourages teens to engage in sexual activity before they reach adulthood. Abstinence is believed to be the best form of contraception and the best way to protect oneself against STDs and STIs. Critics of abstinence-only sex education believe that this is a naïve way of addressing the topic, as most teens will engage in sexual activities before they reach adulthood. Therefore, they argue, it is better to be armed with the right information so they can make the right decision.

Sex education and all the debates around it are not unique to the United States. Can proper sex education help teach people about what consent is? Can it help address rape culture and stealthing? Moreover, what should be done when sex education interferes with religious beliefs? Does it jeopardize the right of a parent to choose when and how their child learns about sex? Those are questions that complicate the issue of sex education.

Those who support sex education believe that it can empower women and girls to have greater autonomy over their body. In addition, sex education is believed to be a public health issue: a crucial step toward decreasing the rate of people being infected with sexually transmitted diseases. The thought process is that if people are informed about the use of condoms and how diseases like HIV are transmitted, they have a better understanding of how to protect themselves and are more willing to do so. The following chapter focuses on the different types of sex education, including the controversies surrounding Planned Parenthood, which provides sex education, among other services.

VIEWPOINT 1

> "As the name implies, Planned Parenthood is not only a woman's organization, it is also a man's organization that increasing numbers of men are beginning to recognize."

Planned Parenthood Has Helped Millions of Women

Maureen Miller

Planned Parenthood is an organization that has been around for more than 100 years but is a target of antiabortion activists because it provides abortions, among many other important health services. In the following viewpoint, Maureen Miller explains that this organization is crucial to women's empowerment as it allows them to have autonomy over their reproductive life. Planned Parenthood has given women access to information to help them make better decisions about their reproductive future. In addition, Planned Parenthood has become increasingly essential to men also because they, too, benefit from its services. Maureen Miller is an infectious disease epidemiologist and adjunct associate professor of Epidemiology at Columbia University.

"How Planned Parenthood Has Helped Millions of Women, Including Me," by Maureen Miller, The Conversation, February 2, 2017. https://theconversation.com/how-planned-parenthood-has-helped-millions-of-women-including-me-71672. Licensed under CC BY-4.0 International.

Is Sex Education a Right?

As you read, consider the following questions:

1. Who founded Planned Parenthood?
2. How is the largest percentile of Planned Parenthood's budget spent?
3. Who is Alan Rosenfield?

Planned Parenthood has allowed generations of low-income women to survive childbirth, to combat sexually transmitted infections (STIs) and to plan their pregnancies. However, the fact that women live healthier and longer lives is not Planned Parenthood's ultimate superpower. No, that is reserved for the legions of low-income women, including me, who now have been given the opportunity to dramatically move up the economic ladder and prosper.

For millions of women, Planned Parenthood is at once a symbol of and a means to women's empowerment. Since the organization helped topple cultural norms that held back women, it's no surprise that men, many of whom feel excluded from this process, grasp familiar though outdated standards to justify defunding it.

Recently, Republican congressional leadership has tied the defunding of Planned Parenthood (along with the repeal of the Affordable Care Act) to the upcoming budget reconciliation bill, which needs only a simple majority of senators to pass. It is hard to say what will happen next. Although all sides acknowledge the odds favor Republican efforts, they also acknowledge that Planned Parenthood will not go down without a fight.

As a public health researcher with expertise in the social factors that influence disease transmission, especially sexually transmitted infections, I think it's important to look at the history and the facts about Planned Parenthood. Many lies have been told about it, and it's important to know the truth.

> ## SEXUALLY TRANSMITTED INFECTIONS ARE PREVALENT
>
> Sexually transmitted infections (STIs) are very common and are caused by infections that are passed from one person to another during sexual contact.
>
> These infections often do not cause any symptoms. Medically, infections are only called diseases when they cause symptoms. That is why STDs are also called "sexually transmitted infections." But it's very common for people to use the terms "sexually transmitted diseases" or "STDs," even when there are no signs of disease.
>
> There are many kinds of sexually transmitted diseases and infections. And they are very common—more than half of all of us will get one at some time in our lives.
>
> The good news is we can protect ourselves and each other from STIs. Practicing safer sex allows you to reduce your risk of getting sexually transmitted infections. And if you've done anything that puts you at risk of infection, getting tested allows you to get any treatments you may need.
>
> "Sexually Transmitted Infections (STIs)," Planned Parenthood Hudson Peconic, Inc.

More Than 100 Years of Promoting Reproductive Health

In 2016, Planned Parenthood celebrated its 100th year of existence. In 1916, Margaret Sanger opened the first Planned Parenthood, a birth control clinic, in Brownsville, Brooklyn to address the hardships that childbirth and self-induced abortions brought to low-income women. She and her colleagues were promptly arrested.

So began the many legal and political battles Planned Parenthood has waged over the control of women's fertility. Yet it was men who had the strongest impact on the social acceptance of birth control at that time. World War I saw the largest global mobilization and deployment of populations in history. Since the populations were almost exclusively young men, this led, not surprisingly, to a massive increase in STIs, then called venereal disease. Suddenly, "birth control" seemed like a really good idea.

In fact, even today the largest percentage (41 percent) of Planned Parenthood's budget is spent on testing and treating STIs, followed by contraceptive services (31 percent) for both women and men. The number of men who receive services such as testing for STIs and checkups for reproductive or sexual health issues from Planned Parenthood has grown steadily and has increased by almost 100 percent over the past decade.

All of these statistics are buried in data-filled documents that are hard to find and daunting to review. But here are some numbers readily available: In 2014 (the most recent year for which complete data are available) Planned Parenthood operated with a budget of US$1.3 billion, more than 40 percent of which came from the federal government (mostly in the form of Medicaid reimbursements). It provided almost 10 million clinical services to about two and a half million patients, the majority of whom were low-income.

Men have lobbied for the inclusion of men in maternal and child health (MCH) programs. Beginning in 1975, Alan Rosenfield, the former dean of the Mailman School of Public Health at Columbia University, established a series of sexual health clinics in Upper Manhattan, including one of the first "Young Men's Health" clinics.

However, it was his groundbreaking and oft-cited piece in The Lancet, "Maternal mortality: a neglected tragedy," that provided influential public support for Planned Parenthood missions to prevent women dying from pregnancy-related complications and the need for family planning.

It is perhaps no surprise that all of this attention on women's sexual rights, combined with the widespread uptake of oral contraceptives—the "pill," the first entirely female-controlled method of pregnancy prevention—found Planned Parenthood once again at the center of a firestorm, of which I was blissfully unaware on my first visit to Planned Parenthood.

Reproductive Rights

A Personal Story

When I was 14 years old, my mother dropped me off at the local Planned Parenthood and told me she'd be back in an hour. Up until that day, she had been the only person willing to answer the myriad questions about sex posed by her breathless and curious all-girl 4-H club, of which I was a member. (I doubt they would have approved her choice of troop leader topics.)

At the time, filmstrips of Roman gods and goddesses with strategically draped fig leaves passed for sex education at our school. Now, my mother had reached her limit. Despite my delusions of sophistication (I was the recent owner of two-inch heeled, cork-bottomed white clogs), the idea that I would actually have sex with someone—with a man!—was the farthest thing from my mind.

As I headed toward the entrance, head down and slump-shouldered, to attend a real sex education class, I searched for the words and the nerve to announce myself to the receptionist. I didn't even have to open my mouth. I was whisked away to a room filled with eight other girls. None of us made eye contact, but my eyes were certainly opened that day.

Did I mention that my mother had me when she was 19 years old?

My mother, who was the first in her family to go to college, did not graduate. I have a Ph.D. I was given the privilege to determine the course and timing of my reproductive life. Though not without bumps, reproductive freedom allowed me to pursue academic and professional dreams. This was an opportunity not afforded to my mother, though one she made darn sure that both my sister and I would have.

Educational Gains: A Connection?

Over the last decade in the U.S., the number of women attending college has greatly eclipsed the number of men attending. This is true across communities: Among Latinos there is a 13 percent point gap in college enrollment between women and men, among African-Americans a 12 percent gap and among whites a 10 percent gap.

The result is economic independence for women, but at social cost. Highly educated women are being urged to date and marry "down," given the dearth of equally educated men. This bucks the traditional norm in which the man is the primary breadwinner and the woman is the stay-at-home mom, a philosophy to which research shows both men and women continue to subscribe.

This cataclysmic shift of women's economic independence, along with rapidly changing demographics in the U.S., has given rise to nostalgia for the "old days" as well as calls to challenge the morality of sexual harassment and discrimination implicitly associated with the old days. Fueling these divergent attitudes is a sense of real frustration on both sides and, perhaps more importantly, an inability to communicate and find common ground.

But there may be ways to take emotion out of the equation, especially for Planned Parenthood. Throughout the history of the organization, men have played an outsized role in support of the Planned Parenthood mission and now make up a larger percentage of patients than ever before.

As the name implies, Planned Parenthood is not only a woman's organization, it is also a man's organization that increasing numbers of men are beginning to recognize. Like parenthood itself, the success of the organization will require the actions and support of both women and men. It's time that men know that they, too, benefit directly from Planned Parenthood.

VIEWPOINT 2

> *"Planned Parenthood facilities offer 18 percent fewer prenatal services now than they did in 2006."*

Four Reasons Why Planned Parenthood Should Be Defunded
Alexandra DeSanctis

Alexandra DeSanctis believes that Republicans have failed to make defunding Planned Parenthood a priority because of fear of repercussion since 62 percent of Americans see Planned Parenthood in a positive light. But she also believes that there are four simple reasons why Planned Parenthood should be defunded. Even though the US abortion rate is declining, the number of abortions performed by Planned Parenthood continues to rise. DeSanctis also believes that besides STD and STI tests, many of the services that this organization provides are on the decline, and that most women do not depend on Planned Parenthood for healthcare access, as the organization claims. Alexandra DeSanctis is a staff writer for National Review and a visiting fellow at the Ethics and Public Policy Center.

As you read, consider the following questions:

1. According to the author, what are the only procedures aside from abortion that have markedly increased at Planned Parenthood clinics since 2006?

"Four Arguments for GOP Politicians Serious About Defunding Planned Parenthood," by Alexandra DeSanctis, National Review, April 16, 2019. Reprinted by permission.

2. What does FQHC stand for, and how many are there in the country?
3. Who is Leana Wen?

Despite the fact that Planned Parenthood remains the largest abortion provider in the United States—performing more than 330,000 abortion procedures last fiscal year alone—the group continues to receive about half a billion dollars annually from the federal government.

For decades, the Republican party has promised to remove that funding, but its efforts continue to fail. There are plenty of complicated reasons for that, as I reported in a recent issue of National Review magazine. But a huge part of the problem is that Republican politicians don't make this goal a central part of their governing agenda, because they believe it would be unpopular.

And they're probably right—a Gallup poll from last summer found that 62 percent of Americans say they have a favorable view of Planned Parenthood.

But if Republican politicians sincerely believe that women deserve better health-care options than Planned Parenthood, and if they truly want to prevent taxpayer dollars from indirectly underwriting procedures that end human lives, they must learn how to educate Americans about why the group doesn't deserve government funding. Here are four easy arguments pro-life politicians should learn how to use:

Planned Parenthood Performs the Most Abortions in the U.S., Even as Our Abortion Rate Steadily Drops

The most recent Centers for Disease Control data indicate that there were about 600,000 abortions in 2015. The Guttmacher Institute, meanwhile, estimates that there are about 900,000 abortions each year in the U.S., accounting for states such as California and Maryland, which don't report their abortion numbers to the CDC (abortion reporting isn't mandatory).

But even as the overall U.S. abortion rate has fallen consistently, if slowly, since the 1980s, Planned Parenthood's share of those abortions has grown. Planned Parenthood's clinics once accounted for about 8 percent of the annual abortions in the U.S. but now account for more than one-third.

Since 1990, the number of abortions performed at Planned Parenthood facilities has more than doubled, from about 129,000 to more than 330,000 last year. That increase has taken place even as the number of women using Planned Parenthood facilities has dropped, from about 3 million a decade ago to 2 million today, as has the overall number of women seeking abortions.

Planned Parenthood Offers Very Few Necessary Health-Care Services, and Most of the Procedures It Does Offer Are on the Decline

Aside from abortion, most procedures offered at Planned Parenthood clinics have declined in number over the last decade. Since 2006, when the group's previous president, Cecile Richards, took the helm, Planned Parenthood's provision of breast-cancer screenings has decreased by more than 65 percent, and its provision of cervical-cancer tests by 75 percent. Over the same period, its provision of reversible contraception declined by 24 percent, and emergency contraception by 54 percent.

Planned Parenthood facilities offer 18 percent fewer prenatal services now than they did in 2006. Their abortion rate, meanwhile, increased by 13 percent. Last year, Planned Parenthood clinics performed 117 abortions for every one adoption referral made. The only procedures aside from abortion that have markedly increased at Planned Parenthood clinics since 2006 were STI and HIV tests.

Women Have Better Health-Care Options than Planned Parenthood

Abortion-rights supporters insist that millions of women rely on Planned Parenthood as their primary source of health care and will be left without any resources if the group is defunded. In reality, there are a variety of options that are better for women than Planned Parenthood.

According to the group's latest annual report, it has "more than 600 health centers" across the nation. Meanwhile, there are more than 13,500 federally qualified health-care centers (FQHCs) and rural health clinics in the United States, outnumbering Planned Parenthood locations 20 to 1.

Data from the Lozier Institute reveal that in California, for instance, there are 114 Planned Parenthood facilities, the most of any state by far. But that is only a small fraction of the nearly 1,700 health centers in the state. New York has 625 FQHCs, but just 58 Planned Parenthood locations. Some states, such as West Virginia, South Dakota, and Mississippi, have only one Planned Parenthood clinic each, but hundreds of FQHCs.

Unlike Planned Parenthood locations, these centers provide comprehensive primary and preventive care—including mental-health and substance-abuse treatment—regardless of an individual's health-insurance status. GOP proposals to remove Planned Parenthood funding are not simply efforts to strip funding from abortion providers; they propose to redirect the entirety of that funding to FQHCs and other centers that provide comprehensive care without performing abortions.

Planned Parenthood Is a Progressive Political-Action Group, Not a Nonpartisan Health-Care Organization

The new president of Planned Parenthood, Leana Wen, has spent the first few months of her tenure insisting that her group has nothing to do with politics and that it cares only about making sure women have access to health care. In reality, Planned Parenthood is one of the most powerful political-action interest groups within the Democratic party, exercising a great deal of influence over left-wing politics and activism.

Every election cycle, Planned Parenthood shells out millions of dollars to elect Democratic politicians who turn around and vote to continue funneling federal dollars to the abortion provider. One recent Planned Parenthood annual report indicated that the group spent about $166 million to, for instance, "promote health equity," spur "movement building," and "strengthen and secure Planned Parenthood"—all code for political activism.

Whenever a state government passes a law restricting abortion in any way, Planned Parenthood is one of the first groups to hit it with a lawsuit. Planned Parenthood executives and activists spearheaded smear campaigns against the nominations of Neil Gorsuch and Brett Kavanaugh, accusing both men of wanting to inflict a "Handmaid's Tale" world on American women. Planned Parenthood is one of the biggest bankrollers of the annual Women's March, which this year came under fire for its leaders' support of notable anti-Semite Louis Farrakhan.

With its bubble-gum-pink banners and slippery slogans, Planned Parenthood has managed to brand itself as a normal health-care provider, convincing Americans that it deserves a blank check from the federal government. But these facts speak for themselves. If Planned Parenthood continues to win this messaging war, it'll be because those who know the truth haven't done enough to bring it to light.

VIEWPOINT 3

> "Planned Parenthood should certainly be defunded, but not because it performs abortions or does anything else that conservatives don't like."

Why Planned Parenthood Should Be Defunded

Laurence M. Vance

According to Laurence M. Vance, the United States government should not be funding Planned Parenthood, an entity focusing on providing reproductive care to mostly women and girls. However, his argument isn't that Planned Parenthood should be defunded because it is the largest abortion provider in the country, as might be expected. Vance believes that Planned Parenthood should be defunded because the United States Constitution does not authorize the funding of private entities. Forty-one percent of Planned Parenthood's revenue comes from government reimbursements and grants. It isn't about alienating Planned Parenthood because of the nature of its services. No private organization and business should be included in the government's budget, the author contends. Laurence M. Vance is a columnist and policy advisor for the Future of Freedom Foundation and an associated scholar of the Ludwig von Mises Institute.

As you read, consider the following questions:

1. What are some of the services provided by Planned Parenthood?

"Why Planned Parenthood Should Be Defunded," by Laurence M. Vance, The Future of Freedom Foundation, July 21, 2017. Reprinted by permission.

2. What is the Hyde Amendment?
3. What are the reasons why the author believes Planned Parenthood should be defunded?

For years now Republicans in Congress have expressed their intention to repeal Obamacare and defund Planned Parenthood. Although they failed to accomplish either goal individually, they came up with the bright idea of introducing a bill that would jointly achieve their objectives.

If it passes.

Because the Republicans had nearly absolute control of the government once Donald Trump was sworn into office, they could have had a bill to repeal Obamacare waiting on his desk in the oval office for his signature on Inauguration Day. A simple one-sentence bill is all that was necessary: "The Patient Protection and Affordable Care Act (PL 111-148, 124 Stat. 119 through 124 Stat. 1025) is hereby repealed."

But because the Republicans were fixated on the need to "repeal and replace" Obamacare instead of just getting rid of Obama's collection of tax increases masquerading as a health-care bill, back in March they introduced a replacement for Obamacare called the American Health Care Act of 2017 (AHCA). Their bill to establish Republicare was withdrawn after the House Republican leadership realized that they did not have enough Republican votes to pass it.

Then, after some tweaking, the House, by a vote of 217 to 213 (20 Republicans and all Democrats voted no), passed the AHCA bill (H.R.1628) on May 4. But instead of acting on the House bill, the Senate came up with its own bill in the nature of a substitute called the Better Care Reconciliation Act of 2017 (BCRA). It has yet to be voted on. Although there are some differences between the two bills, both have identical language ending federal Medicaid reimbursements to Planned Parenthood for one year.

Founded in 1916, Planned Parenthood Federation of America, according to its website,

- delivers vital reproductive health care, sex education, and information to millions of women, men, and young people
- is America's most trusted provider of reproductive health care
- is a respected leader in educating Americans about reproductive and sexual health
- advocates for sound U.S. foreign policies that improve the sexual and reproductive health and well-being of individuals and families globally.

Its mission is

- to provide comprehensive reproductive and complementary health care services in settings which preserve and protect the essential privacy and rights of each individual
- to advocate public policies which guarantee these rights and ensure access to such services
- to provide educational programs which enhance understanding of individual and societal implications of human sexuality
- to promote research and the advancement of technology in reproductive health care and encourage understanding of their inherent bioethical, behavioral, and social implications.

Planned Parenthood has 56 independent local affiliates that operate more than 600 centers across the country. According to Planned Parenthood's most recent annual report, 41 percent ($555 million) of the organization's revenue comes from government reimbursements and grants.

Planned Parenthood is also the nation's largest abortion provider, performing more than 320,000 abortions a year—more than 30 percent of the nation's annual total.

Congressional Republicans want to defund Planned Parenthood because it performs abortions. That, of course, means that the organization has been previously funded. And funded it has been—for years, by Republicans, most recently in the omnibus spending bill (H.R.244) to fund the government for the rest of the fiscal year that was signed into law by Trump on May 5. If Republicans, the vast majority of whom would say they are against abortion, are so opposed to Planned Parenthood because it performs abortions, then why did they fund the organization with millions of taxpayer dollars during the Bush years when they had a majority in both Houses of Congress for more than four years?

Just to clarify, the federal government does not directly fund abortions, except when it does. Congress passed the Hyde Amendment in 1976—three years after the historic *Roe v. Wade* Supreme Court decision that effectively overturned most state abortion laws. It prohibits federal Medicaid coverage of abortions, except when the pregnancy will endanger the woman's life or results from rape or incest. However, it doesn't prevent the states from using their own funds to pay for abortions, and seventeen states do provide abortions to women enrolled in Medicaid. Conservatives argue that because the federal dollars given to abortion providers such as Planned Parenthood are fungible, no abortion provider should be eligible for Medicaid reimbursements, not even for cancer screenings, birth control, or preventive care.

Both the AHCA and the BCRA would cut off federal Medicaid payments to Planned Parenthood for one year (about half of Planned Parenthood patients are on Medicaid) and prohibit most consumers from using tax credits to help buy insurance that includes coverage for abortions.

The bills don't actually mention Planned Parenthood. What they do say is that

> for the 1-year period beginning on the date of the enactment of this Act, no Federal funds provided from a program referred to in this subsection that is considered direct spending for any year may be made available to a State for payments to a prohibited entity, whether made directly to the prohibited entity or through a managed care organization under contract with the State.

The bills define a "prohibited entity" as "an entity, including its affiliates, subsidiaries, successors, and clinics"

(A) that, as of the date of enactment of this Act —
    (i) is an organization described in section 501(c)(3) of the Internal Revenue Code of 1986 and exempt from tax under section 501(a) of such Code;
    (ii) is an essential community provider described in section 156.235 of title 45, Code of Federal Regulations (as in effect on the date of enactment of this Act), that is primarily engaged in family planning services, reproductive health, and related medical care; and
    (iii) provides for abortions, other than an abortion—
        (I) if the pregnancy is the result of an act of rape or incest; or
        (II) in the case where a woman suffers from a physical disorder, physical injury, or physical illness that would, as certified by a physician, place the woman in danger of death unless an abortion is performed, including a life-endangering physical condition caused by or arising from the pregnancy itself; and
(B) for which the total amount of Federal and State expenditures under the Medicaid program under title XIX of the Social Security Act in fiscal year 2014 made directly to the entity and to any affiliates, subsidiaries, successors, or clinics of the entity, or made to the entity and to any affiliates, subsidiaries, successors, or clinics of the entity as part of a nationwide health care provider network, exceeded $350,000,000.

The bills don't block the millions in Title X family-planning funds Planned Parenthood receives annually.

Naturally, the president of Planned Parenthood opposes the bills and has promised intense lobbying to try to defeat or alter them. Cecile Richards said in a statement, "Slashing Medicaid and blocking millions of women from getting preventive care at Planned Parenthood is beyond heartless. One in five women in this country rely on Planned Parenthood for care. They will not stay silent as politicians vote to take away their care and their rights." She also termed the proposed legislation "the worst bill for women's health in a generation."

Planned Parenthood should certainly be defunded, but not because it performs abortions or does anything else that conservatives don't like.

There are three simple reasons why Planned Parenthood should be defunded.

First of all, the Constitution nowhere authorizes the federal government to fund private organizations or businesses that provide services. Here is something that Democrats and Republicans, liberals and conservatives, pro-choicers and pro-lifers should all be in perfect agreement on.

Second, it is an illegitimate function of government to take money from individuals and businesses through taxation and transfer that money to organizations or businesses that provide services—even to nonprofits, even to organizations that don't perform abortions, and even to businesses that provide important services. Businesses should charge for all services they provide and organizations that provide free or low-cost services should be funded by private grants and individual donations. If businesses can't get enough customers and organizations can't get enough grants or donations, then they should close.

Third, if it is okay for a private organization or business to receive government funds for providing family planning, STD testing, or cancer-screening services, then no logical argument can be made against a private organization or business to receive government funds for providing pest-control, auto-repair, hairstyling, house painting, or landscaping services.

It is not just Planned Parenthood that needs to be defunded. All organizations and businesses on the federal dole should be defunded.

VIEWPOINT 4

> "The debate over sex education in schools is not really about whether it's appropriate or not … It's about whether we arm children with the intellectual and emotional tools to stand a chance in it."

Comprehensive Sex Education Can Help Keep Children and Teens Safe

Ian Dunt

In the following viewpoint, Ian Dunt argues that sex education is important because it is the best way to protect young adults. Pornography is everywhere, making it easily accessible to teens. Those images affect the way young girls see themselves and the expectations that young boys have of their sexual partners. Therefore, it is crucial for schools to intervene with sex education programs. Young girls are also prone to be involved in abusive relationships. Young people are exposed to predators and child abusers. In sex education programs, those issues can be addressed. Students can be taught about consent. Ian Dunt is editor-at-large of Politics.co.uk, a regular host on the Oh God What Now podcast, and a a columnist for the New European and the i newspaper.

"Religious Groups' War on Sex Education," by Ian Dunt, politics.co.uk, February 17, 2015. Reprinted by permission.

Reproductive Rights

As you read, consider the following questions:

1. This viewpoint starts with a quote about parents. What does the author believe to be the central problem with the quote's argument?
2. Why do Christian groups oppose comprehensive sex education?
3. How many signatures did the petition led by the Everyday Sexism Project and the End Violence Against Women Coalition receive?

There is a small group of parents, religious groups and predominantly Tory politicians who swing into action every time sex education is mentioned. Today, as the Commons education committee released its report into the subject, they were at it again.

"Parents are the primary educators of their children, they are natural sex educators of their children and they are the experts on their own children," Antonia Tully of Safe at School said. "Parents constantly find themselves having to battle with schools in order to protect their children from inappropriate sex education."

The central problem with this argument is that children cannot be protected from inappropriate material. Online pornography is now so prevalent no child content filter can stop a teenager getting hold of it if they are determined, and generally speaking teenagers are when it comes to pornography.

As Graham Ritchie, principal policy adviser for the children's commissioner, told the committee:

> We know that it affects them. It affects young women and their body image—self-objectification. It affects young men and the expectations that they have of sexual partners. Therefore, it is incumbent on schools to address that issue and talk with young people about it.

Is Sex Education a Right?

Among young girls there are concerning signs they are becoming tolerant of abusive behaviour. Two-fifths of girls said it was acceptable for a partner to make them say where they are all the time and 17% said it was acceptable for their partner to send photos or videos of them without their permission. One in five thought it was OK for them to tell them what to wear.

And then there is the spectre of child abuse. As Alison Hadley, who led the government's successful teenage pregnancy strategy, said, school classes can help protect schools against predators.

> If you have really good, comprehensive sex and relationships education, you talk about consent in a meaningful way with young people. You tell them about age gaps and predatory behaviours, so they start to recognise that. If you are not giving them any ammunition to understand these things, no wonder they are ending up in very dangerous situations.

The debate over sex education in schools is not really about whether it's appropriate or not. The world is full of inappropriate material and behaviour. It's about whether we arm children with the intellectual and emotional tools to stand a chance in it.

But even as today's report was being published, the Daily Mail's front page was whipping up outrage. "NHS gives condoms to pupil aged 13," it screamed. The Mail front page comes from the same emotional place as the Christian groups against sex education— they both approach the world as they would like it to be, rather than as it is. That is not a luxury children themselves have.

And yet the movement against sex education has been remarkably successful, both in Westminster and locally. One primary school said it could not provide the classes because their chair of governors was an elderly priest and "they could not possibly discuss it with him".

The Christian Institute convinced many politicians with claims that primary school sex education classes "often contain graphic material that is highly unsuitable for classroom use" and that "some material is so explicit that if it were shown by an adult to a child in a non-school setting, it would be regarded by many as child abuse".

It was all nonsense. Janet Palmer, national lead for personal, social, health and economic education at Ofsted, said the watchdog had not encountered inappropriate materials.

> What we did find usually were materials that were too little too late—materials that were being used where children were asking these questions probably two or three years before and they were not being answered. We did not come across anything that we would say was too explicit for children who were too young.

These campaigns seem to have had some effect on the government. In 2009, Alisdair Macdonald's independent review recommended making personal, social, health and economic education part of the national curriculum. The proposal was lost at the end of the parliament. When the Department for Education launched a new review in 2011, it was off the table. At its conclusion, it was decided it would remain non-statutory and that "teachers are best placed to understand the needs of their pupils and do not need additional central prescription".

A little later, amendments were proposed in the Lords to make sex education compulsory. It was batted away, but Lord Nash, parliamentary under-secretary for schools, wrote to its supporters setting out the steps the government was taking to improve "expectations of high quality" teaching on the subject.

They were not worth much. It's not as if the coalition government is actively against sex education. You just get the sense their heart isn't in it.

While there was a mention of personal, social, health and economic education in the introduction to the national curriculum, other promises were rather weaker. Nash said an email would be sent to all schools with "a very prominent reminder" that they must publish their provision for the classes. But when the education committee got hold of the email, they found it made no mention of it.

Is Sex Education a Right?

> ## ABSTINENCE CAN BE A BIRTH CONTROL METHOD
>
> Sexual abstinence or sexual restraint is a practice of refraining from some or all aspects of sexual activity for medical, psychological, legal, social, financial, philosophical, moral or religious reasons. Sexual abstinence is generally motivated by factors such as an individual's personal or religious beliefs. Sexual abstinence before marriage is required in some societies by social norms or by laws.
>
> Sexual abstinence could be voluntary when an individual chooses not to engage in sexual activity due to moral, religious, philosophical reasons, or could be involuntary as a result of social circumstances such as when one cannot find sexual partners
>
> Some groups advocate total sexual abstinence, by which they mean the avoidance of all sexual activity, in the context of birth control the term usually means abstinence from vaginal intercourse. Abstinence is 100% effective in preventing pregnancy however is very difficult to practice and not everyone who intends to be abstinent refrains could from all sexual activity
>
> Experts recommend that those using abstinence as a primary method for birth control should have backup method also readily available such as use of condoms or emergency contraceptive pills. Deliberate non-penetrative sex without vaginal sex or deliberate oral sex without vaginal sex is also sometimes considered as a birth control measure. While this generally avoids pregnancy, pregnancy can still occur with intercrural sex and other forms of penis-near-vagina sex such as genital rubbing, and the penis exiting from anal intercourse where sperm can be deposited near the entrance to the vagina and can travel along the vagina's lubricating fluids.
>
> "Abstinence—Birth Control Method," Web Conversion Online.

As the education committee found:

The government's current strategy for improving [sex ed] in schools is weak, and the recent actions taken by the government are insufficient to make much difference.

The committee found personal, social, health and economic education needed improvement in 40% of schools. This is a significant decline since 2010, when provision was good or outstanding in three-quarters of schools surveyed.

Young people consistently report the sex ed they receive is inadequate. There is a dearth of suitably trained teachers or time devoted to the subject.

We know the demand is there. Ninety-eight per cent of Mumsnet users said they were happy for their children to receive sex ed. The National Association of Head Teachers reported that 88% of parents of school-aged children wanted it to be compulsory. A petition led by the Everyday Sexism Project and the End Violence Against Women Coalition calling for classes on sexual consent, respectful relationships and online pornography received over 36,000 signatures. Girlguiding UK said young girls "want and need" the classes.

We just need the supply. And for that we need a government which does not get embarrassed discussing it, or opt instead for technologically illiterate solutions like internet filtering systems. The sooner sex education is put on the national curriculum and given the funding and training it deserves, the sooner we'll have protected our children from the dangers of the internet age.

VIEWPOINT 5

"Excluding consent and sexual agency from our educational objectives has long-lasting, tragic implications."

The Role of Education in Preventing Sexual Misconduct
Laura McGuire

Because we live in a culture that promotes hazy or even wrong images of sex and consent, Laura McGuire argues in the following viewpoint that conversations about consent should start much earlier than adulthood. The author believes that school administrators and teachers should be trained on the subject matter because consent is not a topic that should only be discussed in health classes. It is a topic that constantly needs to be reiterated. Schools need to act against the culture of toxic gender roles and of the high tolerance of abuse that students are constantly subjected to. Dr. Laura McGuire is a nationally recognized sexuality educator, trauma-informed specialist, and inclusion consultant at the National Center for Equity and Agency.

As you read, consider the following questions:

1. What are the top three guidelines offered in the viewpoint for creating cultures of consent in schools?
2. What is rape culture?
3. When does the author believe that consent needs to start being addressed in schools?

"The Role of Education in Preventing Sexual Misconduct," by Laura McGuire, Edutopia, October 25, 2018. All rights reserved. Used with permission.

As a consultant and researcher on sexuality and misconduct, I know that preventing sexual misconduct starts with education that shifts the paradigms and norms we have about sex, relationships, and bodily autonomy.

Adulthood is not the best time to start these conversations—by then, our culture and media have already sent millions of messages in the wrong direction. And making sex and sexuality the enemy is the least effective approach. Research shows that the more we talk about sex and agency in the late childhood and teen years, the less likely it is that abusive dynamics will arise—and, if they do, the more likely that self-efficacy and personal advocacy will be present.

As educators, it's our goal and responsibility to nurture the whole student. Excluding consent and sexual agency from our educational objectives has long-lasting, tragic implications—ones we see, for example, in the scandal that has hit Chicago Public Schools.

Based on my experience as a teacher, trainer, and sex education expert, here are my top three guidelines for creating cultures of consent in our schools.

Discuss Consent in All Its Forms

Consent is not as simple as a cup of tea (as an infamous video would have it). We've all grown up in a culture that promotes assault and harassment—through movies, music, and advertisements, we're fed a steady stream of stories about unhealthy relationships that are presented as romantic, seductive, or humorous. Interpersonal communication continues to follow scripts that promote dishonesty and toxic gender roles—with boys being depicted as sexually insatiable and never victimized, and girls as either "good" and sexually pure, or "at-risk" and hypersexualized.

All of these depictions feed into the concept we call rape culture: the beliefs, myths, and social scripting that promote and maintain sexual violence.

Consent is far more than "no means no," and even "yes means yes" does not cover all the dynamics involved in authentic, affirmative, and enthusiastic consent. Consider the concepts of token resistance (TR) and token compliance (TC). TR is the expectation of a no when the individual really wants to say yes—e.g., "good girls" are supposed to not like sex, and their no supposedly masks their genuine desires. TC is the flip side: a person saying yes under pressure when they'd rather say no. To educate on consent, we must address these points honestly.

School districts and educators can bridge the gap in subject matter competency around the affirmative consent paradigm by bringing in sex education experts. Sexuality and consent are topics that many educators hesitate to bring up because of a lack of resources and understanding of how to address these deeply complex topics appropriately with children, tweens, and teens, and a sex education expert can help.

Having these conversations in health classes where sex and relationships are already discussed is too limiting to create the shift in cultural values that we need to heal the structural inequalities that lead to sexual misconduct and abuse. We need to train all teachers and administrators on sexual misconduct, consent, dating violence, and reporting and response obligations under Title IX. We then need to infuse these conversations across the curriculum so that students receive these messages consistently throughout their school years.

Explain Sexual Agency and Subjectivity

Sexual agency is the ability to assert sexual needs, desires, and boundaries effectively. Sexual subjectivity is an individual's ability to reflect on their sexual needs, identity, and rights to pleasure. Together, these concepts form the foundation for creating cultures of consent.

All communal transformation begins with empowering the individual. We can help students unlearn messages about sexual shame, victim-blaming, and slut-shaming, and teach them about body image, sexual empowerment, and their right to sexual pleasure and autonomy. Doing so can shift the current paradigm. Not including sexual pleasure in the conversations we have in sex education classes, for example, feeds into the cultural norms that lead to sexual abuse.

Promote Healthy Relationships for Everyone

Part of creating a consent culture is exploring what defines a healthy relationship. Any time two or more people are interacting—whether in friendship, flirting and dating, or long-term and marital relationships—both empathy and consent must be present.

Conversations that assume that everyone is cisgender or heterosexual are not the answer, and neither are ones that paint every victim of assault as female (they aren't) and every perpetrator as male (women and girls commit abuse and assault too).

We must break away from these stereotypes and decolonize these discussions. Every culture, ethnicity, and religion has a unique perspective on and expectation for courtship, love, and sex. Ensuring that consent is culturally humble and inclusive is key to guaranteeing its applicability in every community.

We must look critically at whether our depictions of sexuality are centered on straight, white, or cisgendered narratives. If the curriculum or facilitators are focusing on a limited cultural perspective, we should consult with consent educators from other cultures and communities to ensure that messages are inclusive and not resting on a framework of Western moral superiority.

When do we begin this work? As soon as our children can understand language. The seeds of consent are planted in the way we show our children how to share, how to ask before touching or taking, and that every person has the inalienable right to their body.

Our children need to know their right to assert their ability to say no and to require an authentic yes from even those in positions of power. This cannot begin soon enough, because consent is about so much more than sex—it is about the human rights that we are gifted at birth. Schools are in a uniquely important position to do this challenging, grassroots work.

Periodical and Internet Sources Bibliography

The following articles have been selected to supplement the diverse views presented in this chapter.

Gary D Bouma, "Young people want sex education and religion shouldn't get in the way," The Conversation, September 5, 2018. https://theconversation.com/young-people-want-sex-education-and-religion-shouldnt-get-in-the-way-96719

Hayes Brown, "Republicans want sex ed out of schools. That's a huge mistake," MSNBC, May 11, 2022. https://www.msnbc.com/opinion/msnbc-opinion/sex-education-belongs-schools-republicans-want-it-out-n1295332

Katelyn Cordero, and Gary Stern, "'Culture wars' in Dutchess school boards; Why politics have spilled into education," Poughkeepsie Journal, May 12, 2022. https://eu.poughkeepsiejournal.com/story/news/education/2022/05/12/dutchess-school-elections-2022-diversity-equity-critical-race-theory/9585829002/

Georgia Edkins Whitehall, "More than 5,000 parents go to war with Welsh government over plans to teach children as young as THREE about 'sexual attraction' and gender identity," Mail Online, April 24, 2022. https://www.dailymail.co.uk/news/article-10747825/Parents-sue-Welsh-government-plan-teach-children-young-THREE-sexual-attraction.html

Brent Johnson, Matt Arco, and Adam Clark, "New N.J. sex education standards spark belated backlash. Here's what Murphy, Republicans say," NJ.com, April 13, 2022. https://www.nj.com/education/2022/04/nj-adopted-new-sex-education-standards-2-years-ago-theres-now-an-uproar-from-republicans.html

Olga Khazan, "Republicans have sex ed all wrong," The Atlantic, April 14, 2022. https://www.theatlantic.com/politics/archive/2022/04/school-sex-education-grooming-protecting-kids/629556/

Natalia Mehlman Petrzela, "Opinion: SEL doesn't have to be a classroom culture war," CNN, May 13, 2022. https://edition.cnn.com/2022/05/12/opinions/social-emotional-learning-petrzela/index.html

Annie Pena-Castellanos, "Commentary: Trans and queer stories are vital to sex-ed," The Ithacan, May 11, 2022. https://theithacan.org/opinion/commentary-trans-and-queer-stories-are-vital-to-sex-ed/

Sophie Shead, "Sexual assault is not a crime of ignorance: Why consent education does not address the real problem," ABC, April 14, 2022. https://www.abc.net.au/religion/sophie-shead-sexual-assault-is-not-a-crime-of-ignorance/13838672

Trish Zornio, "Zornio: Why is Colorado so hesitant to talk about sex education with kids?" The Colorado Sun, March 28, 2022. https://coloradosun.com/2022/03/28/zornio-sex-ed-opinion/

CHAPTER 3

What Happens When Someone Needs Help Conceiving?

Chapter Preface

Many challenges prevent couples from conceiving a child the traditional way, including infertility. Infertility is a health issue that affects many men and women. It can cause emotional stress and put a strain on a couple's relationship. In many countries around the world, women are sometimes blamed for infertility, even though the husband might be the sterile partner. This is based on a traditional belief that women are largely responsible for procreating simply because they are the ones to carry the child. Being unable to give birth to a child within a marriage can have serious ramifications in those cases, including divorce.

Alternative options like in vitro fertilization, surrogacy, and adoption, exist for couples and individuals who struggle to conceive. Nevertheless, the costs associated with those options can be remarkably high. There are also pros and cons to all options available. Surrogacy, in particular, is a hotly debated form of assisted reproduction.

Many hopeful parents, including celebrities, have turned to surrogacy to bring their child into the world. Advocates for surrogacy stress that it can be a positive experience for the intended mother and surrogate mother. There are many myths surrounding this practice, including a fear that the surrogate mother will claim rights to the child. But, according to advocates, this is very unlikely.

One of the main reasons for pushback against surrogacy is a belief that it exploits women. Critics believe that surrogacy commodifies women's bodies. In India, commercial surrogacy is now banned. The country was one of the largest surrogacy providers in the world. Moreover, because of how costly surrogacy is, it is a practice that is mostly accessible to wealthy hopeful parents.

The cost of alternative options becomes even more of an issue when it comes to same-sex couples. Same-sex couples are already marginalized by the U.S. health-care system. Their right to a reproductive future is often contested, and finding the right access to assisted reproduction is often a challenge.

What Happens When Someone Needs Help Conceiving?

The viewpoints in following chapter will explore the aspects of reproductive health that focus on infertility, other methods of childbearing and conception, and the stigma and challenges that accompany them.

VIEWPOINT 1

> *"There is a tendency of society to blame the woman for failed conception."*

Too Often, Women Are Blamed When a Couple Has Trouble Conceiving

Philip Teg-Nefaah Tabong and Philip Baba Adongo

In the following excerpted viewpoint, Philip Teg-Nefaah Tabong and Philip Baba Adongo argue that women are often blamed when a couple deals with infertility, especially in developing countries. In many countries where there is a high pressure for childbearing, stigmatization can take the form of being ridiculed by the husband's family, being treated as an outcast, and even divorce. When women are infertile, they often experience a lot of shame. Moreover, because, in general, society tends to focus on female factors when a couple has trouble conceiving, there is a lack of data on how men deal with infertility. Philip Teg-Nefaah Tabong is affiliated with Ghana Health Service, Brong Ahafo Regional Hospital in Ghana. Philip Baba Adongo is Department of Social and Behavioural Sciences, School of Public Health, College of Health Sciences, University of Ghana.

As you read, consider the following questions:

1. How does the World Health Organization define infertility?

"Infertility and Childlessness: A Qualitative Study of the Experiences of Infertile Couples in Northern Ghana," by Philip Teg-Nefaah Tabong and Philip Baba Adongo, BioMed Central Ltd, March 21, 2013. https://bmcpregnancychildbirth.biomedcentral.com/s/10.1186/1471-2393-13-72. Licensed under CC BY-4.0 International.

2. What are some of the issues that women face when they are deemed infertile by their community?
3. How do men's and women's reactions to infertility differ?

Infertility has been defined as failure to conceive after one year of regular unprotected sexual intercourse in the absence of known reproductive pathology [1]. However, epidemiological studies have revealed that in a normal population of heterosexually active women who are not using birth control, 25% will become pregnant in the first month, 63% within 6 months, and 80% within one year. By the end of a second year, 85% to 90% will have conceived [2]. Because some couples, who are not infertile, may not be able to conceive within the first year of unprotected sex, the World Health Organisation therefore recommends the epidemiological definition of infertility, which is the inability to conceive within two years of exposure to pregnancy [1]. Infertility may be primary or secondary. Primary infertility refers to infertility of a woman who has never conceived and secondary infertility refers to infertility of a woman who has conceived at least once before. The use of the ability of the female to conceive as a measure to differentiate between primary and secondary infertility is however problematic as it places responsibility for a couple's infertility on the doorsteps of the female partner.

Worldwide, more than 70 million couples suffer from infertility, the majority being residents of developing countries [3]. Developing countries experience negative consequences of childlessness to a greater degree when compared with Western societies [4]. Regardless of the medical cause of infertility, women receive the major blame for the reproductive setback and they suffer personal grief and frustration, social stigma, ostracism and serious economic deprivation [5]. In Cameroon, infertility is a reason for divorce among the Bangangte tribe, causing a woman to lose her access to land distributed by her husband [6]. In Egypt, women go through a complicated ritual known as kabsa (a form of fertility-producing ritual) in efforts to overcome infertility [7]. Among the Ekiti of Southwestern Nigeria, infertile women are treated as outcast, after they die, and their bodies are buried on the outskirts of the town with those of people experiencing mental ill-health [8].

In view of the importance attached to parenthood in Africa, it is not surprising that infertility is reported to be considered a major cause for divorce and marital instability [9, 10]. Consequently, infertile women commonly fear abandonment, divorce and polygamy [5, 11]. In Northern Ghana, it is customary for the families of both the bride and groom to expect the announcement of an expected baby within a year of marriage and any delay in the signs of pregnancy by the woman is unacceptable [12]. The ability of the woman to give birth is generally viewed as a gain to the family of the woman's in-laws for the bride wealth paid to the family of the woman.

There is a tendency of society to blame the woman for failed conception [13]. Consequently, the accepted norm is that infertility in a couple stigmatises the wife as barren and the husband as sterile. In this manner the implication of sterility presents men with an opportunity to abandon barren wives and de-stigmatise themselves by opting out of childless marriages. Participants' in a study conducted in Cape Town indicated that they had to deal with being called Idlolo, meaning barren and stjoekoe (failure) [5]. Traditional customs, such as having to wear a scarf until a woman has a child also contributes to more pressure on women who suffer from infertility. In a study in South Africa, women expressed that they felt especially stigmatized and ridiculed in their families and in their communities. Participants described how they were sworn at, shouted at, cursed and victimized, seeing themselves as outcast, especially within their husbands' families [5]. Prior to the realisation of involuntary childlessness, the individual probably identifies him or herself as a normal, conforming member of society [14]. It may be therefore, that social reaction to the disclosure of infertility plays a part in the establishment of a stigmatised identity. Women regard childlessness as discreditable, negative, and as representing failure. In addition, most experienced anxiety, isolation, and conflict as they privately explore the possibility of personal infertility. To avoid feelings of personal inadequacy, many women exclude themselves from gatherings such as baby showers or avoid their pregnant friends prior to revealing their involuntary childless status [14].

Studies have also revealed that the inability to have a child is often devastating to both partners; however, there are differences in men and women's reactions to infertility. Prior research has tended to concentrate on the woman's experience while virtually ignoring the men [15]. Another study indicates that both sexes experience strong feelings of sorrow, isolation, urgency, guilt, and powerlessness [15]. Nevertheless, as a rule these feelings are generally expressed differently. In general, women are verbal and tend to seek out support during times of stress, while men use avoidance, minimisation, and denial. Contrarily, infertility has some positive effects in marriage such as bringing partners closer in the search for a solution to their problem. In a longitudinal cohort study of 2, 250 people who started fertility treatment, 25.9% of women and 21.1% of men were reported to have benefited [16]. Another study found that Muslim participants disclosed that they were afraid their husband might take a second wife. This is allowed by their religion so long as the first wife gives her blessing. However, this blessing is not required from a woman who cannot conceive [5]. In conclusion, women seem to submit to what they perceive as the consequence of infertility.

The treatment for infertility can either be traditional or biomedical. Traditional infertility services are common in Africa, and have been reported by many scholars and proponents of traditional medicine. Traditional health care is an important alternative source of understanding, coping, and managing health problems, including infertility, in the Gambia [17]. Medical therapy on the other hand is used to correct ovulation dysfunction (irregular or infrequent periods). If there are no underlying causes of ovulation problems (such as a thyroid disease), the first line of treatment is oral medication to induce regular menstrual cycles. For ovulatory dysfunction, representing almost 20% of female infertility [18], Clomiphene Citrate (CC) can initiate ovulation. Ovulation is induced in 50–70% of cases and, together with timed intercourse, the pregnancy rate varies between 15 and 25% per cycle with a low multiple pregnancy rate of 6–8% [18]. Surgery is sometimes required to treat conditions associated with infertility. The vast majority of surgical procedures used to address infertility can now be performed on an outpatient basis using a laparoscope (a type of endoscope) inserted through the navel and assisted reproduction technologies. For males, low sperm counts, deformed spermatozoa and inability to sustain an erection (impotence) are managed using medication. From the literature, there appears to be a gender bias in research on management of infertility as many studies have often focused on the women, reinforcing the belief that infertility is mainly caused by female factors.

[…]

References

1. WHO: Infections, pregnancies, and infertility: perspectives on prevention. Fertil Steril. 1987, 47: 964-968.
2. National collaboration centre for women and children health: Fertility: Assessment and treatment for people with fertility problems. 2012, London: RCOG, 20.
3, Fathalla MF: Reproductive health: a global overview. Early Hum Dev. 1992, 29: 35-42. 10.1016/0378-3782(92)90055-L.
4. Sundby J, Mboge R, Sonko S: Infertility in the Gambia: frequency and health care seeking. Soc Sci Med. 1998, 46: 891-899. 10.1016/S0277-9536(97)00215-3.
5. Dyer SJ, Abraham N, Hoffman M, Van der Spy ZM: Infertility in South Africa: women's reproductive health knowledge and treatment-seeking behaviour for involuntary childlessness. Hum Reprod. 2002, 17: 1663-1668. 10.1093/humrep/17.6.1663.

6. Feldman-Savelsberg P: Plundered kitchens and empty wombs: fear of infertility in the Cameroonian grassfields. Soc Sci Med. 1994, 39 (4): 463-474. 10.1016/0277-9536(94)90090-6.
7. Inhorn MC: Interpreting infertility: medical anthropological perspectives. Soc Sci Med. 1994, 39 (4): 459-461. 10.1016/0277-9536(94)90089-2.
8. Ademola A: Change in the patterns of marriage and divorce in a Yoruba town. Rural Africana. 1982, 14: 16-
9. Leke RJ, Goyaux N, Matsuda T, Thonneau PF: Ectopic pregnancy in Africa: a population-based study. Obstet Gynecol. 1993, 103 (4): 692-697.
10. Sundby J: Infertility in the Gambia: traditional and modern health care. Patient Educ Couns. 1997, 31: 29-37. 10.1016/S0738-3991(97)01006-9.
11. Dyer SJ: The value of children in African countries: insight from studies on infertility. J Psychosom Obstet Gynaecol. 2007, 28 (2): 69-77. 10.1080/01674820701409959.
12. Banga EH: Traditional practices affecting the health of women and children in Africa. The Nurse-Educator Bulletin. 1989, 7: 3-9.
13. Bharadwaj A: Culture, infertility and gender–vignettes from South Asia and North Africa. Sexual Health Exchange. 2002, 2 (14): 6-9.
14. Miall C: Perceptions of informal sanctioning and the stigma of involuntary childlessness. Deviant Behaviour. 1986, 1 (6): 383-403.
15. Phipps S: Men and women react differently to infertility. South Africa Today. 1993, 122 (2581): 14-17.
16. Schmidt L: Social and psychological consequences of infertility and assisted reproduction: what are the research priorities?. Hum Fertil. 2009, 12 (1): 14-20. 10.1080/14647270802331487.
17. Wischmann T, Stammer H, Scherg H, Gerhard I, Verres R: Psychosocial characteristics of infertile couples: a study by the Heidelberg fertility consultation service. Hum Reprod. 2001, 16: 1753-1761. 10.1093/humrep/16.8.1753.
18. Ombelet W, Cookes I, Dyer S, Serour G, Devroey P: Infertility and the provision of infertility medical services in developing countries. Hum Reprod. 2008, 14 (6): 605-621. 10.1093/humupd/dmn042.

VIEWPOINT 2

> "[Surrogacy] can also be a positive experience when undertaken with appropriate societal support and when all participants practice mutual respect, kindness and empathy."

Becoming a Parent Through Surrogacy Can Be a Positive Experience

Danielle Tumminio Hansen

Surrogacy is often viewed as an ethically challenging route to bringing a child to life. Many celebrities have chosen to bring their future child to life through surrogacy, including Gabrielle Union and Nicole Kidman. Some of the concerns that author Danielle Tumminio Hansen states in the following viewpoint include a lack of regulations, the potential effect on the child, possible exploitation, and the cost of the procedure. There are also a lot of myths and fears that prevent people from getting the right information about surrogacy. Nevertheless, Hansen believes that when done correctly, surrogacy is a blessing for couples struggling to conceive. Danielle Tumminio Hansen is Assistant Professor of Practical Theology & Spiritual Care at Emory University's Candler School of Theology.

"Becoming a Parent Through Surrogacy Can Have Ethical Challenges—but It Is Positive Experience for Some," by Danielle Tumminio Hansen, The Conversation, October 6, 2021. https://theconversation.com/becoming-a-parent-through-surrogacy-can-have-ethical-challenges-but-it-is-a-positive-experience-for-some-167760. Licensed under CC BY-4.0 International.

As you read, consider the following questions:

1. What is the difference between "traditional surrogacy" and "gestational surrogacy?
2. What is reproductive trauma?
3. What year did India ban international surrogacy?

In her new book, actress Gabrielle Union became the latest celebrity to discuss her decision to become a parent via surrogacy. She joins the ranks of household names such as Neil Patrick Harris, Nicole Kidman, Kim Kardashian, all of whom have hired a surrogate to give birth to their future child.

The publicity Union generated about surrogacy reignited ethical questions about this controversial form of assisted reproduction that range from whether women should be able to sell their reproductive abilities to what it means to be a parent.

There is global disagreement about the ethics of surrogacy. Several countries have banned it, while others have limited its scope. In the United States, laws permitting surrogacy vary by state.

The legal range is due to ethical concerns, ranging from the potential exploitation of surrogates to worries that surrogacy negatively affects the life of the resulting child.

In the decade that I've been researching this form of assisted reproduction, I've discovered that surrogacy can be exploitative, but it can also be a positive experience when undertaken with appropriate societal support and when all participants practice mutual respect, kindness and empathy. At its best, it can also encourage people to adopt a more expansive view of what it means to be a family.

Myths and Fears

One could argue that the concept of surrogacy dates back to a biblical story in the book of Genesis in which Sarah, the wife of Abraham, pleads with him to have children with the slave Hagar because of Sarah's inability to conceive.

Reproductive Rights

TYPES OF SURROGACY

There are many different ways to define surrogacy—by the way the embryo is created, by whether the surrogate is compensated or not, by which professional you work with, and so much more! Here are just a few different types of surrogacy to define:

Gestational Surrogacy: the family planning option in which a woman (surrogate) carries and delivers a child for a couple or individual. In gestational surrogacy, the surrogate (or gestational carrier, or GC) carries a child conceived of the egg and sperm of two other individuals and is therefore not biologically related to the child.

Traditional Surrogacy: the family planning option in which a woman (surrogate) agrees to carry a pregnancy for an intended parent or parents and in which the surrogate is genetically related to the baby. In traditional surrogacy the surrogate's eggs are used, making her the biological mother of the child she carries. Because this, in turn, creates emotional and legal issues, traditional surrogacy has been banned across the U.S. and is no longer recognized as a form of surrogacy.

Commercial or Compensated Surrogacy: any surrogacy arrangement in which the surrogate mother is compensated for her services beyond reimbursement of medical expenses.

Altruistic Surrogacy: any surrogacy arrangement in which the surrogate mother is NOT compensated for her services beyond reimbursement of medical expenses.

Agency Surrogacy: any surrogacy arrangement in which the intended parents and/or gestational carrier work with a licensed surrogacy agency.

Independent Surrogacy: sometimes called private surrogacy is any surrogacy arrangement in which the intended parents and surrogate mother do not work with a surrogacy agency.

Identified Surrogacy: any surrogacy arrangement in which the intended parents already have a gestational carrier in mind when beginning the surrogacy process. Often, it is a family member or close friend.

"Types of Surrogacy," Adoption Surrogacy Choices of Colorado.

Fast forward to modern times, and surrogacy is now performed predominantly in high-priced in vitro fertilization centers in one of two ways. In "traditional surrogacy," the fertilized egg belongs to the surrogate. In "gestational surrogacy," which is more common today, the fertilized egg comes from either the intended mother or a donor. In both cases, that egg combines with a sperm to become an embryo that grows in the surrogate's womb and not the intended mother's.

Gestational surrogacy may be preferable because it allows intended mothers to maintain a genetic connection with their child. Others may prefer it because of fears that a surrogate could lay claim to the child with whom she had a biological connection.

The fear that a surrogate will try to steal or adopt a child is one of many legal and ethical fears surrounding surrogacy. In the 1980s, the Baby M Case in the United States attracted much media attention because it tapped into these fears. In this situation, the surrogate named Mary Beth Whitehead attempted to retain custody of the baby she birthed.

The case fueled a stereotype of surrogates as emotionally unstable, defying the reality that surrogates undergo psychological testing before participating in a procedure.

Documented instances of surrogates retaining children are rare. Research shows that surrogates often experience pregnancy and birth differently than they did with their own children. They also often see themselves as heroes or gift givers instead of mothers.

If the public perceives surrogates negatively, intended parents often fare no better. They are often categorized as selfish, desperate and filthy rich, especially when they choose surrogacy without a medical reason.

Those popular images of intended parents fail to account for the reproductive trauma many of them experience prior to turning to surrogacy. Psychologists have shown that the inability to start a family can be a form of reproductive trauma. The decision to hire a surrogate, then, is often the last option for parents who have tried everything else. What is seen as desperation, in other words, is actually, as I've proposed in my own research, an attempt to write a happy ending to the story of their reproductive lives.

Ethical Concerns About Surrogacy

It is true that this way of becoming a parent is expensive, at least in the United States, where use of the technology routinely costs over US$100,000. The cost is so extreme because intended parents pay health care fees for both themselves and the surrogate, many of which aren't covered by insurance.

They also have to pay legal fees, agency fees, and compensate the surrogate, which alone can range from $45,000 to $75,000. Contrast that price tag to one in India prior to its ban on international surrogacy in 2015: Couples who traveled there could expect to spend between $15,000 to $20,000 in total for their surrogacy journey.

The extreme costs of surrogacy in the U.S. limits its availability to the wealthy and to high profile celebrities like Union, raising important ethical questions about whether this is an appropriate use of resources, especially given the possibility of adopting.

In addition to ethical questions about surrogacy's relation to wealth, feminists are divided on how surrogacy affects women. Some feminists feel that surrogates have a right to choose what to do with their bodies. Others object to surrogacy on the grounds that systemic oppression drives women into surrogacy; or that it's unethical for women to sell their bodies, arguing that it parallels prostitution.

Cases documented in India support these concerns. Investigative journalist Scott Carney found one prominent Indian surrogacy clinic where surrogates were kept in crowded bedrooms on restricted diets and forced to have caesarean sections in order to streamline the labor and delivery process.

Scholars also worry about surrogacy's impact on children. Studies suggest that children of surrogates may struggle with their identity, especially if those children are not told of their origins.

Extensive research hasn't been conducted with children of surrogates. Research by social scientists studying children born via egg and sperm donation largely mirrors the findings of adoption research: Children have questions about their identity, and answers to these questions are often most accessible when children have access to those individuals who are part of their birth story. Yet agencies and governments rarely regulate how surrogates, intended parents and children interact following the baby's birth.

Finally, many religious groups, most prominently Roman Catholics, object to surrogacy because it results in the destruction of human embryos during IVF cycles and violates their theological conviction that life begins at conception. Roman Catholics encourage heterosexual couples who cannot procreate via intercourse to adopt as an alternative.

The Case for Surrogacy

Such objections might lead to the conclusion that there is never a reason to hire a surrogate. But this might be too simplistic. Even with the documented struggles on the parts of both intended parents and surrogates, many are profoundly grateful for the technology.

Intended parents often feel surrogates are "gifts from God" who help them reach their dream of parenthood. Meanwhile, some surrogates believe their powers of procreation provide them with a unique opportunity to help others. Many surrogates see their ability to create life as a source of power, a profound act of altruism and part of their legacy.

When I spoke with a group of surrogates in Austin, Texas, while conducting research for my book, I found that their stories aligned with the findings of other researchers who discovered that many surrogates had positive experiences in which they experienced themselves as heroes. These women felt empowered because they helped infertile heterosexual couples and gay couples create families. Without surrogacy, these individuals would have no way to have a genetic connection with their children.

The surrogates acknowledged that sometimes intended parents could be difficult, that pregnancy and labor could be challenging, and that it could be confusing when a checkout clerk at the grocery store asked what they were planning to name the baby.

Becoming a parent through surrogacy can, as Union explains, be awkward and humbling, confusing and miraculous all at the same time.

But when surrogates and intended parents can act freely, out of a sense of religious calling and with the support of society, then there is the potential for them to discover that family is not just biological but also social and relational. In those encounters, many experience the technology as life-giving, both metaphorically and literally.

VIEWPOINT 3

"Expanding access to reproductive services could lead to an increase in exploitation, health risks and the further commodification of women's bodies."

A Global Approach to Surrogacy Is Needed to Stop Exploitation of Women

Herjeet Marway and Gulzaar Barn

Commercial surrogacy is banned in the United Kingdom and India. Both countries opted for an unpaid, altruistic approach to surrogacy. India is in the process of banning international commercial surrogacy and allowing surrogacy to only take place between parties inside the country. In the following viewpoint, Herjeet Marway and Gulzaar Barn argue that there is still more that needs to be addressed. Surrogacy, the authors contend, exploits women. The change of law in India still leaves loopholes that can be exploited by surrogacy clinics. Moreover, the change in how the World Health Organization defines infertility could further exasperate the demand

"Surrogacy Laws: Why a Global Approach Is Needed to Stop Exploitation of Women," by Herjeet Marway and Gulzaar Barn, The Conversation, July 30, 2018. https://theconversation.com/surrogacy-laws-why-a-global-approach-is-needed-to-stop-exploitation-of-women-98966. Licensed under CC BY-4.0 International.

Reproductive Rights

As you read, consider the following questions:

1. Who are the largest consumers of the Indian commercial surrogacy industry?
2. How much money does surrogacy bring to the Indian economy?
3. Besides India, what other country could be considered a hot spot for commercial surrogacy?

Surrogacy may have become a popular way for many couples in the limelight to have children—notably Kim and Kanye, Elton John and David Furnish, as well as Sarah Jessica Parker and her husband Matthew Broderick. But it isn't just a service for the rich and famous.

People may choose to use a surrogate for all sorts of reasons—fertility issues being the obvious one—but people with health problems or complications with previous pregnancies as well as same-sex couples or single people looking to start a family, are all also common clients.

In the UK, altruistic (unpaid) surrogacy is legal, but commercial (paid) surrogacy is not. At present, however, Britons are the largest consumers of the Indian commercial surrogacy industry.

Surrogacy is reported to bring in US$400m every year to the Indian economy. But the Indian market has come under fire for being exploitative. Indian surrogate mothers are typically poor, and are paid around £4,500 to carry a foetus to term.

The industry is also unregulated. This gives surrogacy clinics a large amount of power and control over the process. Many surrogates are required to live in surrogacy hostels, run by clinics, for the duration of their pregnancy—away from friends and family members.

A Change in the Law

India is in the process of outlawing commercial surrogacy in favour of an altruistic model, available to Indian nationals only. And surrogacy laws in the UK may also be set to change.

The Law Commissions of England and Wales, and Scotland, recently commenced a three-year project to review and recommend improvements to surrogacy arrangements in the UK. One key area targeted for reform is the way in which uncertainty in the law may be encouraging UK residents to look overseas for surrogates.

It may not be enough for countries to amend their laws in isolation. Improvements of national laws are of course welcome, but a collective international response is preferable. This is because, even if the Indian bill passes—and the UK maintains its altruistic approach—this does not fix the problem.

Surrogacy agencies in India and elsewhere could make use of loopholes that exist in the law. Eggs, sperm, embryos, surrogates and intended parents could simply be moved across borders to countries where commercial surrogacy is not banned. What's more, when one industry closes, another one can easily open elsewhere. This is the case in Ukraine, which is fast becoming a surrogacy hot spot now that other countries have banned the practice.

Defining Infertility

Another factor to consider in all of this, is the World Health Organisation's proposal to change the definition of infertility. This would move it away from a clinical disease-based definition—where it is viewed as a disability—to a view that includes a more social definition, recognising it as a "right to reproduce."

Under the new definition, infertility would no longer be seen as "the failure to achieve a clinical pregnancy after 12 months or more of regular unprotected sexual intercourse." Rather, it would also be considered to include cases when "single men and women without medical issues ... do not have children but want to become a parent."

As yet, the proposed definition has not been officially adopted by the WHO. In fact, the WHO has stated that it will retain a clinical focus and refrain from making recommendations about fertility service provision—even if there were to be a change to its definition.

Hypothetically, the result of this change would mean that those who fall under the new social account of infertility could also receive access to reproductive services. On the one hand, this is a progressive move—why shouldn't single men and women and same-sex couples receive help to become parents?

But on the other hand, there are concerns that the expanded definition ignores the gender dynamics inherent to the provision of reproductive services.

A Right to a Womb

Any change in the law needs to recognise that it is women's bodies alone that can perform this "service." In the case of male gay couples, who cannot carry a foetus themselves, women's bodies will be necessary in order to treat a couple's infertility. This could be either through international paid surrogacy, or the domestic altruistic model.

If this definition does take hold, there may well be an increase in the demand for surrogacy services and the further liberalisation of surrogacy laws to cater for this demand. Expanding access to reproductive services could lead to an increase in exploitation, health risks and the further commodification of women's bodies. And without proper acknowledgement that it is women who will carry out the labour involved in gestating a child, a key ethical concern is neglected.

This is why there needs to be an international consensus on surrogacy—and a joined-up approach to the law. There may well be difficulties in getting people from different places, cultures or backgrounds to agree the demand for and effects of current surrogacy practices, but surrogacy deserves a global conversation.

VIEWPOINT 4

> "There are ... no federal requirements that sperm banks obtain and verify information about a donor's medical history, educational background or criminal record."

Sperm Donation Must Be Regulated

Naomi Cahn and Sonia Suter

Sperm donation is unregulated. The last time Congress took action regarding assisted reproductive technology was 1992. States have begun to intervene, with Washington requiring the disclosure of donor-identifying information and medical history as soon as the child turns 18, and Connecticut enacting a law in January 2022 requiring fertility clinics to collect identifying information from donors. It's true that some of those laws might raise the cost of fertility treatments, but in the following viewpoint Naomi Cahn and Sonia Suter argue that there are ways to cut costs and that those laws are vital to help hopeful parents make the right choice for their reproductive future. Naomi Cahn is Professor of Law at University of Virginia. Sonja Suter is Professor of Law at George Washington University.

As you read, consider the following questions:

1. Why did Wendy and Janet Norma sue Xytex Corp.?
2. What is the Uniform Parentage Act?

"Sperm Donation Is Largely Unregulated, but That Could Soon Change as Lawsuits Multiply," by Naomi Cahn, Sonia Suter, The Conversation, January 18, 2022. https://theconversation.com/sperm-donation-is-largely-unregulated-but-that-could-soon-change-as-lawsuits-multiply-174389. Licensed under CC BY-4.0 International.

Reproductive Rights

3. What would the pending New York bill require of sperm and egg donor banks?

When Wendy and Janet Norman decided to have a baby, they went sperm shopping through Xytex Corp., a sperm bank.

The couple chose Donor #9623. Xytex, the Normans later claimed, told them the man spoke multiple languages and was pursuing a doctorate.

Xytex had also assured them that it carefully screened all donors by reviewing their family health history and criminal records and that it subjected donors to intensive physical exams and interviews to verify the information.

But after Wendy Norman gave birth to a son in 2002, the couple learned their child had inherited a genetic blood disorder for which Wendy was not a carrier. He would, much later, require extended hospitalizations because of suicidal and homicidal thoughts.

Even later, they learned that the donor, James Christopher Aggeles, had lied to the sperm bank about his background and that the sperm bank had not verified the information he provided. Nor did it make him supply his medical records or sign a release that would have made it possible to obtain them.

As law professors who study reproductive technology, we see this case and others like it as showing why the government should tighten regulations over sperm and egg donation so that prospective parents and donor-conceived adults receive accurate and complete details about their donors' medical, academic and criminal history.

A 'Wrongful Birth'?

Aggeles wasn't pursuing an advanced degree when he began donating sperm. He didn't even have a college degree at that point. He also failed to disclose his diagnosis of schizophrenia, a severe mental health condition requiring lifelong treatment. Schizophrenia has a high level of heritability in families. He had also been arrested at the time of his donation and was later incarcerated for burglary.

When the Normans sued Xytex, a local court initially dismissed almost all claims in their case. They appealed to Georgia's Supreme Court, which in 2020 allowed several of their claims to go forward.

The Normans could, for instance, seek financial compensation, partly to cover the additional expenses they might have avoided had they learned about the donor's medical history sooner. The court also told the Normans they could try to recover the price difference between what they paid for the sperm they received and its market value.

Finally, the Normans were allowed to allege under the state's Fair Business Practice Act that the sperm bank had misrepresented to the public the quality of its sperm and its screening process.

The Supreme Court of Georgia did not, however, permit the couple to sue over what is known as a "wrongful birth" claim. These claims are negligence actions brought by parents based on the birth of a child with disabilities or genetic disorders because of a provider's failure to identify the risk.

The case is still pending.

Limited Regulation

The Normans' lawsuit is hardly unique.

Other families have sued sperm banks after having donor-conceived children who wound up with a variety of genetic disorders.

In many of those cases, the sperm banks said they routinely test sperm and exclude donors who could pass along genes that cause genetic diseases. In those instances, the families have grounds for accusing the sperm banks of fraud and negligence.

Some donor-conceived adults are also suing doctors who lied to the plaintiffs' parents about whose sperm they were receiving and instead used their own. Several states now ban this kind of "fertility fraud."

This litigation is on the rise because of the growing popularity of direct-to-consumer DNA testing, which makes it easier to identify previously anonymous sperm donors and to learn about genetic risks donor-conceived people may have inherited from them.

It's also happening because of the absence of clear rules and laws regulating sperm banks. There is little regulation of reproductive technologies of any kind, including in vitro fertilization, a procedure that fertilizes the egg with sperm in the laboratory instead of the body, at the state or federal level.

Because the government does not track artificial insemination, the number of donor-conceived people is unknown.

The federal government requires only that donated sperm and eggs be treated like other human tissue and tested for communicable diseases—infectious conditions that spread through viruses, bacteria and other means—but not genetic diseases.

There are also no federal requirements that sperm banks obtain and verify information about a donor's medical history, educational background or criminal record.

What Is the Basis for These Lawsuits?

The allowable grounds for fertility negligence vary by state.

Some states let families sue clinics that fail to screen donors, even when the parents seek damages associated with the birth of the child with a dangerous genetic condition. This would essentially allow a wrongful birth claim to go forward.

But a growing number of states, at least 14 so far, prohibit such claims. That is leading many courts, like the Supreme Court of Georgia, to define the injury as distinct from the birth of the donor-conceived child.

The End of Anonymity

One complication in terms of resolving these disputes is that most sperm donations are anonymous.

At odds with the donor's interest in keeping their identity a secret, we argue, are donor-conceived people's strong interests in learning about their donors, including their medical, educational and criminal history—and even identity.

DNA tests, including direct-to-consumer kits like 23andMe, are rendering donor anonymity impossible to maintain. And internet searches, as the Normans discovered, can make it possible to see whether a donor, once identified, has misrepresented their personal information.

States Are Beginning to Set Rules

Because Congress has taken no action regarding assisted reproductive technology since 1992, states have slowly begun to step in.

In 2011, Washington required the disclosure of donor-identifying information and medical history when a child turns 18.

On Jan. 1, 2022, Connecticut enacted the Uniform Parentage Act, which is based on model legislation drafted by a national nonpartisan commission to fill widespread legislative gaps. The measure requires that fertility clinics collect identifying information from donors and indicate whether donors have agreed to disclosure.

Another pending measure in New York would require sperm and egg donor banks "to collect and verify medical, educational and criminal felony conviction history information" from any donor. That legislation would also provide prospective parents who purchase eggs or sperm and donor-conceived people with the right to obtain such information without personally identifying the donor. This option could make it possible to preserve donor anonymity, at least theoretically.

The bill was drafted at least partially in response to the experience of Laura and David Gunner, whose donor-conceived son died of an opioid overdose. After their son's death, the Gunners learned that a few years earlier, the donor himself had died and that he had been diagnosed with schizophrenia. The donor had not disclosed his mental illness or hospitalizations for behavioral issues.

Costs Are Not a Barrier

It's possible that measures like the one pending in New York state would make fertility treatment somewhat more expensive.

Currently, a vial of donor sperm may cost close to $1,000, with the donor often being paid up to $150.

Genetic testing, however, might not add much to the cost because it would only be done once, rather than each time a patient obtains a vial of sperm. With artificial insemination, it's rare for a pregnancy to occur on the first or second try.

As we learned from Tyler Sniff, an advocate for the New York bill and a director of the nonprofit U.S. Donor Conceived Council, DNA testing companies offer relatively inexpensive options that can cost less than $300.

To be sure, disclosure requirements might overpromise how much prospective parents can learn about their future children. But we are certain that these issues will become even more critical as technology continues to outpace its regulation—and as both donor-conceived adults and an increasing number of people who used sperm banks advocate for their interests.

VIEWPOINT 5

> *"...[Gamete] donors have good reasons to claim a right to certain types of information about the offspring conceived by their donations."*

Donors Are Not Entitled to Information About Children Conceived from Their Gametes

Inez Raes, An Ravelingien, and Guido Pennings

In the following excerpted viewpoint Inez Raes, An Ravelingien, and Guido Pennings share arguments that donors can use to be granted access to their offspring's information. In the past two decades, many countries have moved away from anonymous donations to open-identity donations to help donor-conceived children find more information about their identity. The authors believe that the donors should be taken into consideration as well, as information about their offspring could be vital to them too. The authors are professors in the Department of Philosophy and Moral Science at Ghent University, Belgium.

"The Right of the Donor to Information About Children Conceived from His or Her Gametes", by Inez Raes, An Ravelingien and Guido Pennings, Oxford Academic, January 12, 2013. Reprinted by permission.

2. What are the five arguments that donors can use to gain information about their offspring?
3. Beginning in 2009, what kind of information did donors have rights to in the UK?

The field of gamete donation for medically assisted reproduction purposes is evolving. While anonymous gamete donation was long the preferred practice, a new focus on the rights and interests of donor-conceived children has led a number of countries to shift towards an open-identity system. However, this evolution appears to overlook whether information exchange could also be of interest to the other parties involved, in particular the gamete donors. In this article, we analyse the question whether donors should be granted a right to some information about the offspring conceived by their donations. We constructed five arguments which donors could use in support of such a claim: (i) It can be of great importance to the donors' and their own children's health that they receive medical information (in particular, evidence of an unsuspected genetic disease) about the donor offspring; (ii) basic information (such as whether any children were born) could be a way to acknowledge donors for their altruistic behaviour; (iii) general information (information about the child's wellbeing) about the donor offspring could ease the donors' potential concern about and sense of responsibility for the offspring; (iv) basic information could provide an important enrichment of the donors' identities; (v) identifying information would be useful for donors who want to contact the donor offspring.

[…]

Introduction

Over the past two decades, there has been a remarkable trend towards more openness in the practice of gamete donation. While initially only anonymous donation was permitted, 11 jurisdictions, such as Sweden, Finland, The Netherlands, UK, New Zealand and a number of Australian states have shifted towards an open-identity system (Janssens et al., 2011). In these countries, donors are no longer allowed to donate anonymously. Instead, they have to consent to the release of their identity to the children conceived from their gametes if they request this once they become mature.

This shift towards open-identity donation is the result of a new focus on the rights and interests of donor-conceived children (Scheib and Cushing, 2007). However, this evolution appears to focus exclusively on this party. Policy-makers seem to overlook whether information exchange could also be of interest to the other parties involved, in particular the gamete donors. As it stands today, donors rarely receive information about the result of their donation. A few countries make an exception to this. In the UK, since 2009, donors are granted access to anonymous information about the number of children born from their donation, their sex and year of birth (Human Fertilisation and Embryology Authority, 2009). In Victoria and New Zealand, donors can even receive identifying information about their donor-conceived children, but only if the donor-conceived child consents (New Zealand Government, 2004; Victorian Registry of Birth Death and Marriages, 2008).

Apart from these exceptions, the possible interests and rights of donors are not taken into account. Therefore, it would be useful to scrutinize the donors' perspective on the practice of gamete donation. We need to analyse the question, "do donors also have an interest in receiving some kind of information about the offspring conceived by their donations and do they consequently have a right to such information?"

Possible Arguments in Favour of the Donor
[…]

We identify five arguments on which donors could base their claim for a right to some type of information about the offspring conceived by their donations: In what follows, we will analyse these arguments and evaluate the weight of the underlying interests.

- Medical information, in particular evidence of an unsuspected genetic disease, about the donor offspring can be of great importance to the donors' and their own children's health.
- Donors should be acknowledged for their altruistic behaviour. Basic information is a minimal reward for their donation.
- General information about the donor offspring should be given as a means to ease the donors' potential concern about and sense of responsibility for the offspring.
- Basic information can provide an important enrichment of the donors' identities.
- The open-identity system creates a 'new' type of donor—one that desires contact with the donor offspring. Identifying information enables such contact.

[…]

Conclusion

Our analysis shows that gamete donors have good reasons to claim a right to certain types of information about the offspring conceived by their donations. Information about genetic disorders can be important for the donors' and their own children's health. Basic information about the offspring can also be regarded as an appropriate reward for their altruistic behaviour. Such information can also play a role in the enrichment of their identity by confirming their procreation. Moreover, general information about the child's wellbeing can be an important way to reassure concerned donors. Finally, it can be argued that a possibility to get in touch should be offered when all parties involved agree. While the provision of various degrees of anonymous information about the donor offspring should thus be considered, we have not found strong arguments in defence of a right to identifying information about the donor offspring.

Viewpoint 6

> "It's estimated that, in the United States, there are almost one million frozen embryos now in storage."

Infertility Grief Continues with Decisions over Leftover Embryos

Juli Fraga

In the following viewpoint, Juli Fraga argues that, although IVF has become a popular option for those struggling to conceive, a moral and ethical quandary has arisen that was not foreseen when the technology was first introduced. Many couples and individuals who find success with IVF are left with a several additional embryos, which they must decide whether to destroy, store, or donate. Most are unprepared for the deep emotions that arise when confronting their options. Juli Fraga is a journalist covering mental health and wellness. Her work can be found in The New York Times and The Washington Post, among others.

As you read, consider the following questions:

1. What options are given to people who have frozen embryos stored at fertility clinics?
2. Why might someone feel guilt, anxiety, and sadness over deciding what to do with leftover embryos?
3. What can fertility clinics do to prepare couples who use these services for potential emotional trauma?

"After IVF, Some Struggle with What to Do with Leftover Embryos," by Juli Fraga, NPR.org, August 20, 2016. Reprinted by permission.

Reproductive Rights

When Scott Gatz and his husband decided to become fathers several years ago, pursuing parenthood meant finding both an egg donor and a surrogate to help them conceive a baby. Their first round of in vitro fertilization produced seven healthy embryos. One of those embryos was successfully transferred to their surrogate's womb, resulting in their son Matthew, who is now 6-years-old.

While the San Francisco couple feels their family is now complete, they are still in a quandary over what to do with their six remaining embryos—what they call their "maybe babies."

Every year they're forced to weigh their options again, Gatz tells Shots, when a letter arrives from the fertility clinic. It asks whether they want to destroy the embryos, donate them for medical research, give them to another infertile couple or continue paying $800 annually to keep the embryos frozen.

"Every time we read the 'destroy' option on the form, my stomach does a somersault," Gatz says. "It feels as if our future children are showing up once a year to confront us."

The men are not alone in their ambivalence. It's estimated that, in the United States, there are almost one million frozen embryos now in storage, a number that includes embryos reserved for research, as well as those reserved to expand families.

In a 2005 study that interviewed 58 couples who conceived through IVF and had at least one frozen embryo in storage, more than 70 percent had not yet decided—even several years after the procedure—how they would dispose of a surplus embryo. Some said they considered the embryos to be biologic tissue or a genetic or psychological "insurance policy." Others told the researchers they thought of the embryos as living entities—"virtual children" that have interests that needed to be considered and protected.

"With the astonishing advancements in reproductive science, IVF now produces far more embryos than it did in the past," says Dr. Anna Glezer, a psychiatrist at the University of California, San Francisco. The choices that abundance poses are very difficult for some couples, she says, "which raises the need for psychological resources, such as peer support groups for these families."

After conceiving their daughter via IVF, Megan and Jay Khmelev had eight remaining embryos. For two years, says Megan, she was overcome by guilt, anxiety, and sadness as she struggled with what to do with them. At the beginning of her fertility journey, she had imagined one day donating the embryos to science or to another infertile couple.

But after her daughter arrived, she says, she couldn't imagine parting with the surplus embryos in this way. The Khmelevs didn't want eight more children, but discarding the embryos didn't feel like the right choice, either.

"I wish someone had told me that I'd be haunted by the grief of my infertility struggle all over again as I wrestled with my decision," Megan says.

Dr. Aimee Eyvazzadeh, a reproductive endocrinologist in the San Francisco Bay area, says many families she counsels struggle with these choices.

"It's a complicated process," Eyvazzadeh says. "At the beginning of IVF, patients hope for many embryos, because they long to have a baby. They don't realize how their feelings might change once their children are born."

In the 1980s, when fertility clinics began freezing embryos, there wasn't any available research about how patients would feel regarding their frozen embryos after they became parents. More than 30 years later, though the number of IVF babies has steadily climbed, many fertility doctors are still unsure how to handle some patients' ambivalence.

"Our clinic told us that we could freeze our embryos and explained the cost associated with yearly storage fees," Gatz says, "but they didn't mention the feelings that might arise as we faced these choices."

A study published in the March issue of the journal Fertility and Sterility found that that after successful IVF treatment, most of the 131 couples responding to a survey were dissatisfied with the education they obtained from their health care providers about disposal decisions. And less than 50 percent were satisfied with the emotional guidance they got.

Yet other research suggests that peer support can help people make these complicated choices, by giving them a place to disclose their struggles in the company of others who have been through the process.

Francine Lederer, a clinical psychologist in private practice in Los Angeles, offers a "disposition support group," specifically aimed at couples and individuals who are deciding what to do with their embryos.

"After successful IVF treatments, many couples come to view their embryos as human life, which makes it even harder for them to find closure," Lederer says. Some even have funeral ceremonies for the embryos.

For other couples, making these decisions ignites emotional conflict between the spouses, or even beyond—to include the extended family, Lederer finds, because religious beliefs and personal preferences play a role in how each person views the stored embryos. One couple she counseled who had decided to destroy the embryos mentioned that to their parents and discovered the in-laws were aghast.

"Too often, these families have never shared their stories aloud," says Lederer. "Support groups can make a difference by allowing them to talk about their personal experiences with others who understand, which can help them to feel less isolated."

Megan and Jay Khmelev finally decided to do additional rounds of IVF, and use the remaining embryos themselves, but none resulted in a viable pregnancy.

"I'm glad I did the transfers anyway," Megan says. "It gave me and my husband closure, knowing that we had given them a chance to become life."

Periodical and Internet Sources Bibliography

The following articles have been selected to supplement the diverse views presented in this chapter.

Agence France-Presse in Paris, "French parliament votes to extend IVF rights to lesbians and single women," The Guardian, June 29, 2021. https://www.theguardian.com/world/2021/jun/29/french-parliament-votes-to-extend-ivf-rights-to-lesbians-and-single-women

Irene Caselli, "How Italy's new draconian bill on surrogacy twists the meaning of 'women's dignity,'" WorldCrunch, May 13, 2022. https://worldcrunch.com/opinion-analysis/surrogacy-feminism

Nick Coltrain, "Colorado lawmakers want to make it easier for same-sex parents to adopt their own kids," The Denver Post, March 22, 2022. https://www.denverpost.com/2022/03/22/colorado-same-sex-parents-adoption-legislature/

Susan Dominus, "The nightmare of being a surrogate mother in the Ukraine war," The New York Times, May 4, 2022. https://www.nytimes.com/2022/05/03/magazine/surrogates-ukraine.html

Editorial Team, "Male infertility: causes, treatment and stigma associated with it," TheHealthSite.com, May 7, 2022. https://www.thehealthsite.com/pregnancy/infertility/male-infertility-causes-treatment-and-stigma-associated-with-it-878920/

Korin Miller, "The first fertility treatments that led to IUI and IVF advancements have a deeply disturbing history," Women's Health, May 11, 2022. https://www.womenshealthmag.com/health/a39957791/fertility-treatment-iui-ivf-history/

Chukwuma Muanya, "Experts urge communities to empower infertile women," The Guardian, May 5, 2022. https://guardian.ng/features/experts-urge-communities-to-empower-infertile-women/

Meghan Schultz, "'Rent-a-womb': Priyanka Chopra and Nick Jonas' choice highlights how surrogacy financially exploits women," National Catholic Register, February 1, 2022. https://www.ncregister.com/news/rent-a-womb-priyanka-chopra-and-nick-jonas-choice-highlights-how-surrogacy-financially-exploits-women

Michael Wilner, "Supreme Court decision may hinder access to IVF, a revolutionary fertility tool of the Roe era," McClatchy DC, May 6, 2022. https://www.mcclatchydc.com/news/politics-government/white-house/article261123547.html#storylink=cpy

Claire Wolters, "Same-sex couples face insurance discrimination for fertility treatments," VeryWell, November 18, 2021. https://www.verywellhealth.com/fertility-treatment-same-sex-couple-discrimination-aetna-5210121

OPPOSING VIEWPOINTS® SERIES

CHAPTER 4

What Reproductive Health Concerns Do Women Face?

Chapter Preface

The majority of issues under the umbrella of reproductive rights are experienced by women. Examples of reproductive issues that women face include restricted or costly access to menstrual hygiene products, fear of retaliation by employers when pregnant, postpartum depression, and cost of childcare. This chapter will focus on women's general reproductive health and how some of the topics around women's reproductive health are challenged.

The central controversy around menstrual hygiene products is their expense. In the United States and elsewhere, period pads and tampons are often taxed. And even without the tax, menstrual hygiene products can be costly. For homeless women and girls, for example, the expense can push these products out of reach. Advocates are working to eliminate the sales tax imposed on sanitary products, arguing that they are a necessity, not a luxury. Some countries around the world have made sanitary products free of charge or have removed the tax in order to increase access to them.

Besides sanitary pads, another big issue that women face regarding their menstrual cycle is stigma and period pain. Some companies have started to accommodate women who suffer from severe period pain with period leave, however critics argue that this move might set women back.

Menstrual periods are indeed a subject that is a stigma in many societies. It's often a source of joke in pop culture. In India, women are barred from certain religious activities when menstruating.

Women's reproductive health is often a big issue in the workforce. Women who are mothers are often discriminated against, as employers believe that they are unable to dedicate as much time to their work. Pregnant employees are often viewed as a liability to companies. Paid parental leave is still a debated topic in the United States, where it is not a guaranteed right. How many weeks should mothers be given for parental leave? How long does it take for a woman's body to heal after giving birth? Should fathers take parental leave as well? Those are questions that still need to be addressed.

Lastly, postpartum depression is a highly stigmatized mental illness. Many women suffer from depression after giving birth, and unfortunately it often goes untreated.

VIEWPOINT 1

> *"Barriers for LGBTQ people specifically related to sexual and reproductive health care include systemic infringements on their dignity and right to access health care, and those often play out in the legal and policymaking realm."*

LGBTQ People Need and Deserve Tailored Sexual and Reproductive Health Care

Ruth Dawson and Tracy Leong

According to Ruth Dawson and Tracy Leong, the United States continues to fail the LGBTQ community and ignore the challenges they face in terms of reproductive care. Members of the LGBTQ community are disproportionally affected by reproductive care challenges. Organizations should start by recognizing that reproductive care for LGBTQ patients is not a one-size-fits-all plan, as those who identify as members of the LGBTQ community do not make up a monolithic population. Though many organizations have started to recognize the different reproductive care options that need to be offered, there is still a lot left to be addressed. Ruth Dawson and Tracy Leong are affiliated with the Guttmacher Institute.

"Not Up for Debate: LGBTQ People Need and Deserve Tailored Sexual and Reproductive Health Care," by Ruth Dawson and Tracy Leong, Guttmacher Institute, November 16, 2020. Reprinted by permission. https://www.guttmacher.org/article/2020/11/not-debate-lgbtq-people-need-and-deserve-tailored-sexual-and-reproductive-health

As you read, consider the following questions:

1. What are some of the leading sexual and reproductive health associations that have begun to integrate reproductive and sexual health for LGBTQ patients into their policies and guidelines?
2. What are some of the sexual and reproductive health disparities that LGBTQ patients experience?
3. How does a lack of cultural competency affect LGBTQ patients?

All people, including those who identify as lesbian, gay, bisexual, transgender and queer (LGBTQ), need sexual and reproductive health care. LGBTQ health issues and sexual and reproductive health care are inextricably linked, because they both involve individuals' autonomy in their most intimate decisions. Unfortunately, the health care system in the United States has historically failed and largely continues to fail the LGBTQ community, as LGBTQ people experience major disparities in sexual and reproductive health care and worse health outcomes than the population overall. These differences are due to a series of barriers in the health care system, including fragmentation of health services, discrimination from providers and insurance issues, all of which can be exacerbated by racism and intersecting oppressions. Fortunately, sexual and reproductive health care providers can and do help to address these barriers, taking steps to make tailored, appropriate and lifesaving reproductive health care a reality for millions of LGBTQ people across the country.

Sexual and Reproductive Health Needs

LGBTQ people need and deserve excellent sexual and reproductive health care. Those who identify as LGBTQ are not a monolithic population, and people within that community have different needs, experiences with barriers and levels of access to care.

Sexual and reproductive health care services are crucial components of a holistic picture of health care for LGBTQ people. In particular, all people who are capable of becoming pregnant—which may include queer women, transmasculine people and nonbinary people—may have a need for full-spectrum pregnancy, family planning and abortion care.

A Guttmacher study estimated that several hundred transgender and nonbinary individuals obtained abortions nationally in 2017, primarily at facilities that did not provide transgender-specific health care. LGBTQ people may also need care related to infertility and assisted reproductive technologies, and transgender women and men may have a need for fertility preservation services. Further, LGBTQ people may need STI and HIV testing and treatment; mammograms, Pap smears and other services related to reproductive cancers; screening and support for intimate partner and sexual violence; and gender-affirming services.

Several leading sexual and reproductive health associations have recognized these needs and have begun to integrate reproductive and sexual health for LGBTQ patients into their policies and guidelines. For example, the "Providing Quality Family Planning Services" guidelines set by the Centers for Disease Control and Prevention and U.S. Department of Health and Human Services Office of Population Affairs call for a person-centered approach that integrates the needs of LGBTQ patients. The American College of Obstetricians and Gynecologists has adopted a number of position statements on transgender health, which call for providers to create a welcoming environment for transgender patients and introduce the concept of gender-affirming care. However, these guidance documents for providers have room for expansion in emphasizing contraceptive services and other reproductive health care for LGBTQ patients. Recently, the Society of Family Planning published clinical recommendations on contraceptive counseling for transgender and gender-diverse people, recognizing the need for a tailored approach to contraceptive services for these patients.

Sexual and Reproductive Health Disparities

LGBTQ patients experience disparities in sexual and reproductive health care and outcomes. A recent study suggests that queer people who can get pregnant (except lesbians) are more likely than their straight counterparts to have an unintended pregnancy, a pregnancy when younger than 20 or an abortion, a finding that may suggest structural barriers to contraceptive care and a need for LGBTQ-inclusive comprehensive sex education. Research has shown that lesbian and bisexual women are less likely than straight women to perceive themselves as being at risk of acquiring STIs, a perception associated with minimized use of preventive reproductive health services.

Other research has found queer women do not access routine preventive screenings for breast cancer and cervical cancer at the same rate as their straight peers. These differences in perception and action regarding sexual and reproductive health services can lead LGBTQ individuals to have fewer diagnoses and treatments than their straight counterparts.

The COVID-19 pandemic may exacerbate the disparities LGBTQ people already experience. A recent Guttmacher study found that 46% of queer women reported pandemic-related delays or cancellations of contraceptive or other sexual and reproductive health care compared with 31% of straight women. The study also found that queer women were more likely than straight women to report wanting to delay childbearing or have fewer children.

Barriers to Care

The health care system in the United States has historically failed and largely continues to fail LGBTQ people, with LGBTQ patients experiencing health disparities across the lifespan because they face multiple, and often compounding, barriers to accessing appropriate care. Barriers for LGBTQ people specifically related to sexual and reproductive health care include systemic infringements on their dignity and right to access health care, and those often play out in the legal and policymaking realm.

At the individual level, there are flaws in how the health care system is structured and how health care providers and institutions operate in the forms of a fragmented system, discrimination and lack of provider training, and insurance barriers that impede access for LGBTQ patients, particularly those who face multiple layers of oppression.

Lack of Integration in Health Care

There is fragmentation across the U.S. health care system, and services for LGBTQ people are often separated from sexual and reproductive health care due to structural and funding divisions as well as harmful heteronormative assumptions. (A heteronormative worldview centers straight people and relationships, such as by assuming that queer women do not need birth control.) As a result, LGBTQ people often do not receive comprehensive sexual health counseling, screenings or care, because providers assume they do not need certain services or information.

When it comes to LGBTQ patients, health care systems and providers have historically prioritized HIV/AIDS prevention and treatment, which largely centers men who have sex with men, and more recently have focused on gender-affirming care for transgender people. These types of care are crucial, but do not represent the whole picture of sexual and reproductive health care that LGBTQ individuals need.

Although many leading organizations have made progress in identifying the importance of sexual and reproductive health care for LGBTQ patient populations, significant guiding documents exist that do not meaningfully address this topic. Among these is the World Professional Association for Transgender Health's globally authoritative 120-page "Standards of Care" document, which dedicates a scant page and a half to reproductive health guidance.

Discrimination and Lack of Cultural Competency

The health care system is unfortunately rife with anti-LGBTQ discrimination: Majorities of queer and transgender patients report having experienced discriminatory treatment by health care professionals, and nearly a quarter of transgender patients have delayed seeking health care because of the fear of being mistreated. The health care sector broadly struggles with, but in many ways is working to address, issues of cultural competency—"the ability of systems to provide care to patients with diverse values, beliefs and behaviors," according to the American Hospital Association.

Many sexual and reproductive health care providers have good intentions yet lack cultural competency and training to adequately address LGBTQ patients' needs and make them feel comfortable in a medical setting. Stories abound of LGBTQ patients having bad experiences while seeking sexual and reproductive health care. For instance, providers often give contraceptive counseling based on their assumptions about a patient's sexual behavior, and noncontraceptive benefits of birth control may not be taken into account.

These biases undermine LGBTQ patients' contraceptive care by assuming they are not at risk for pregnancy or STI transmission. Untrained providers also may fail to address a particular concern for transmasculine and nonbinary patients about how hormonal birth control containing estrogen or progesterone may interact with gender-affirming testosterone, and whether testosterone alone is a contraceptive (it is not).

Lack of cultural competency goes beyond the exam room. The vast majority of queer and transgender youth do not see themselves reflected in sex education—only 7% of LGBTQ students report receiving sex education that includes positive representations of both sexual orientation and gender identity topics.

Insurance Barriers

In general, LGBTQ patients are more likely than straight patients to be uninsured. Even patients who have health insurance and visit medical providers who provide competent care may still face insurance denials because of gender markers in their patient profile. For example, an insurer could deny coverage for a transmasculine person seeking birth control because contraceptive care does not align with what the insurance plan categorizes as "male" or "men's" health services.

Intersecting Oppressions

People who experience intersecting oppressions have worse health outcomes overall than those who do not. Barriers to obtaining sexual and reproductive health care can be high for LGBTQ people who are Black, Indigenous or other people of color, those with disabilities, immigrants and those who are low income, as they face layers of systemic marginalization. In the Guttmacher study on early impacts of the COVID-19 pandemic on reproductive health, unpublished data from the small number of queer women in the sample showed that more women of color than White women reported wanting to delay or reduce childbearing and having to delay or cancel sexual and reproductive health care, including contraceptive care.

Moving Forward

There is much more work to be done to ensure that LGBTQ people have the resources, information and care they want and need from a culturally competent, affordable, affirming, inclusive and accessible sexual and reproductive health care system. But there are signs of progress. Increasingly, health care providers and administrators are integrating sexual and reproductive health care for LGBTQ patients into their practices in order to break down silos and ensure access to excellent care. One such promising step is family planning providers increasingly offering gender-affirming care, such as hormone therapy, to their patients. In recent years, state policymakers and advocates have also championed policies and curricula to implement LGBTQ-inclusive sex education.

The sexual and reproductive health field still has work to do. Provider associations should revisit and more meaningfully integrate sexual and reproductive health care for LGBTQ patients into their positions, guidelines and policies. Providers should continue service delivery innovations—such as telehealth or app-based care—that have expanded and accelerated access to gender-affirming services. Sexual and reproductive health care organizations should continue to adopt gender-inclusive language to demonstrate they are welcoming and experienced in serving LGBTQ patients. Individual health care practitioners should adopt an inclusive approach by offering culturally competent, unbiased care, rooted in the understanding of barriers that exacerbate health disparities for LGBTQ people.

Health care for LGBTQ people and sexual and reproductive health care are both constantly scrutinized, criticized, withheld and stigmatized—largely for ideological reasons—and while each faces unique challenges, they are closely linked by a shared value of bodily autonomy. Sexual and reproductive health advocates must stand in support of LGBTQ patients and ensure they receive health care that is tailored for their individual and unique needs.

VIEWPOINT 2

> *"Modern methods of contraception have a vital role in preventing unintended pregnancies."*

High Rates of Unintended Pregnancies Linked to Gaps in Family Planning Services

World Health Organization

The World Health Organization (WHO) believes that unintended pregnancy leads to many issues, including health risks and even death. This viewpoint is based on a study done by WHO in 2019, which revealed that two-thirds of sexually active women in the 36 countries studied had stopped using contraception even though they planned to delay or limit childbearing. Because of that, one in four pregnancies were unintended in those countries. This becomes an issue as it further pushes many women into poverty and increased incidents of malnutrition and other illnesses. Therefore, WHO recommends services to help women and girls access modern contraceptive methods and effective counseling. The World Health Organization is a specialized agency of the United Nations responsible for international public health.

As you read, consider the following questions:

1. Why were sexually active women who wanted to delay or limit childbearing stopping the use of contraception?

Reproduced from WORLD HEALTH ORGANIZATION (WHO), "High rates of unintended pregnancies linked to gaps in family planning services: New WHO study," ©2022. https://www.who.int/news/item/25-10-2019-high-rates-of-unintended-pregnancies-linked-to-gaps-in-family-planning-services-new-who-study. Reprinted by permission.

2. Why does WHO consider unintended pregnancies a public health issue?
3. What kind of services does WHO recommend to address unintended pregnancies?

A new study conducted by the World Health Organization (WHO) in 36 countries found that two-thirds of sexually active women who wished to delay or limit childbearing stopped using contraception for fear of side effects, health concerns and underestimation of the likelihood of conception. This led to one in four pregnancies being unintended.

Whilst unintended pregnancies do not necessarily equate to pregnancies that are unwanted, they may lead to a wide range of health risks for the mother and child, such as malnutrition, illness, abuse and neglect, and even death. Unintended pregnancies can further lead to cycles of high fertility, as well as lower educational and employment potential and poverty—challenges which can span generations.

A Need for High Quality Family Planning Services

Modern methods of contraception have a vital role in preventing unintended pregnancies. Studies show that 85% of women who stopped using contraception became pregnant during the first year. Among women who experienced an unintended pregnancy leading to an abortion, half had discontinued their contraceptive methods due to issues related to use of the method such as health concerns, side effects or inconvenience of use.

Many such issues could be addressed through effective family planning counselling and support.

"High quality family planning offers a range of potential benefits that encompass not only improved maternal and child health, but also social and economic development, education, and women's empowerment," explained Dr Mari Nagai, former Medical Officer for Reproductive and Maternal Health at WHO's Western Pacific Regional Office, and an author of the report.

Unintended pregnancies remain an important public health issue. Globally, 74 million women living in low and middle-income countries have unintended pregnancies annually. This leads to 25 million unsafe abortions and 47 000 maternal deaths every year.

Findings and Recommendations

The WHO study found 4794 women who had an unintended pregnancy after they stopped using contraception. 56% of the women who became pregnant were not using a contraceptive method in the 5 years prior to conceiving. 9.9% of women with an unintended pregnancy indicated that the last method that they had used was a traditional method (e.g. withdrawal or calendar-based method), 31.2% used a short-acting modern method (e.g. pills and condoms) and 2.6% long-acting reversible methods of contraception (e.g. intrauterine device (IUD) and implants).

The study's findings highlight the need for services that:

- take a shared decision-making approach to selecting and using effective methods of contraception that most fit the needs and preferences of clients;
- identify early when women and girls are having concerns about the method they are using;
- enable women and girls to change modern methods while remaining protected through effective counselling and respect of their rights and dignity.

Missed Opportunities to Support Women's Contraceptive Choice

A related WHO study, recently published in the Philippines, found that only 3% of women wanting to delay or limit childbearing received contraceptive counselling during their last visit for any reason to a health facility. Screening all women for family planning concerns could help prevent the large numbers of unintended pregnancies and unsafe abortions occurring in many countries in Asia. In the Philippines alone, it is estimated that there are almost 2 million unintended pregnancies each year and over 600,000 unsafe abortions.

Without adequate counselling, improved quality of service, expansion of effective and acceptable contraceptive choices and respect for the rights of all women and girls, the cycle will continue. Equity is also an important concern. The recent Philippines study showed that women with the least education who did not want to be pregnant were one-third as likely to use modern contraceptives as the most educated.

"Access to high-quality, affordable sexual and reproductive health services and information, including a full range of contraceptive methods, can play a vital role in building a healthier future for women and girls, as well as contributing to attainment of the Sustainable Development Goals," said Dr Ian Askew, Director of the Department of Reproductive Health and Research at WHO.

Ensuring More People Benefit from Modern Contraception

Overcoming legal, policy, social, cultural and structural barriers will enable more people to benefit from effective contraceptive services. A key component of such services will be firstly, to identify women who may have concerns about their method of contraception and wish to switch methods; and secondly, to provide high-quality counselling, free of stigma, discrimination or coercion to those women in order to ensure that their reproductive intentions are respected, and their sexual health protected. It is also essential to improve the skills of doctors, nurses and midwives through training and professional development, so that they can provide effective family-centred counselling to all women who need it.

VIEWPOINT 3

> "Women of color need comprehensive health care—not just to protect their health but also to protect their economic security."

The Affordable Care Act Is Essential for the Reproductive Health of Women of Color

Heidi Williamson

In the following viewpoint Heidi Williamson argues that repealing the Affordable Care Act (ACA) would disproportionately harm women of color because it has allowed marginalized women to gain access to healthcare. Among the benefits of ACA is better access to reproductive health care. Women of color face more challenges when it comes to reproductive health, including a higher rate of unplanned pregnancy, cervical cancer, and maternal mortality. Williamson notes that Congress pushed to have ACA repealed despite the gains it offers to women of color. Though three bills introduced by Congress failed to pass, there has been a consistent effort to remove the Affordable Care Act. Heidi Williamson is the senior policy analyst for the Women's Health and Rights Program at the Center for American Progress.

As you read, consider the following questions:

1. What are the three congressional bills that aimed to repeal ACA?

"ACA Repeal Would Have Disproportionately Harmed Women of Color," by Heidi Williamson, Center for American Progress, August 15, 2017. Reprinted by permission.

2. What is the rate of unintended pregnancies for Latina and Black women?
3. How would the three congressional bills affect the reproductive health care of women of color?

Women of color have benefited immensely from the Affordable Care Act (ACA). Through the ACA, coverage for women of color grew at more than twice the rate of women overall between 2013 and 2015. Of particular importance is the ACA's role in addressing women of color's reproductive health needs, both through its requirement for insurers to cover 10 essential health benefits and provide no-cost preventive services and through its option for states to expand Medicaid. As a result, the uninsured rates among black women, Asian American and Pacific Islander (AAPI) women, and Latinas have declined significantly, and women of color have increased their regular usage of a doctor's office, clinic, or health center.

Yet despite this progress, conservatives in Congress recently waged an all-out assault on health care with little regard for the impact it would have on women of color. Three congressional repeal bills—the House-passed American Health Care Act (AHCA), the Senate's Better Care Reconciliation Act (BCRA), and the Senate's so-called skinny repeal bill—failed to become law but nonetheless threatened to reverse the gains attained through the ACA for millions of women of color and their families.

After it became clear that neither the AHCA nor the BCRA could muster sufficient support to reach the president's desk, the Senate made a last-ditch effort to pass the skinny repeal bill, legislation that would have repealed part of the ACA without a replacement bill. That measure did not pass the Senate, in a dramatic vote in which three Republicans—Sens. Lisa Murkowski (AK), Susan Collins (ME), and John McCain (AZ)—voted no. All of these bills would have harmed women of color and exacerbated already pervasive health disparities.

Women of Color Face Extraordinary Health Disparities

Historically, women of color have faced significant obstacles regarding their access to reproductive health care. As a result, health disparities and racial biases are still prevalent, even with the gains achieved through the ACA. While unintended pregnancy rates are down overall, the rates for Latinas and black women still outpace the rate for white women: The rate of unintended pregnancies for Latinas is 58 percent, and the rate for black women is 79 percent—more than double the 33 percent rate for white women. The pregnancy-related mortality rate for black women is more than triple the rate for white women.

Further, black women ages 45 to 64 have the highest rates of breast cancer and maternal mortality, while Latinas have the highest rates of cervical cancer. Cancer is also the leading cause of death for AAPI women. Women of color have higher rates of pre-existing conditions such as diabetes, asthma, hepatitis B, and HIV/AIDS—and because of the coverage gap, they are more likely to die from these conditions. The coverage gap applies to states without Medicaid expansion, where people's incomes are too high to qualify them for Medicaid but not high enough for them to participate in the ACA marketplace. All these conditions would be exacerbated if women of color were locked out of health care coverage.

Generally, communities of color experience worse health care outcomes because of income inequality, barriers to care, lack of insurance, and lack of a consistent medical provider. Women of color are also more likely to be underinsured, uninsured, and eligible for Medicaid. If women of color live in states where Medicaid has not been expanded to cover more individuals and families, they are more likely to receive lower-quality care, especially if they are low-income. And many women of color currently fall into the coverage gap, particularly in states where Medicaid has not been expanded, and they remain uninsured. Despite the significant drops in the uninsured rates among black, Latina, and AAPI communities, these systemic barriers continue to lead to health care disparities.

Key Similarities and Differences Among the Repeal Bills

The three versions of the ACA repeal bills share key similarities that could threaten reproductive health care for women of color: repealing individual and employer-mandated coverage and defunding Planned Parenthood. First, all three bills would have repealed the provision in the ACA that requires most individuals to purchase insurance, often referred to as the individual mandate. Without the mandate, many individuals would likely opt out of the market, causing a sharp increase in premiums. The resulting decline in outreach efforts would also lead to fewer people being insured and lower Medicaid enrollment. Passage of the AHCA would have resulted in 24 million people losing coverage by 2026; passage of the BCRA would have resulted in 22 million people losing coverage in the same time frame. The skinny repeal bill—an ill-conceived option pitched as a streamlined repeal effort by targeting the individual and employer mandates and the medical device tax—still would have resulted in 16 million people, including many women of color, becoming uninsured. And although it would not have cut Medicaid, premiums for those with private insurance would have increased by 20 percent, making insurance unaffordable for many women. The Center for American Progress estimates that this would have cost individuals $1,238 in higher premiums. All three bills would have resulted in millions of women of color losing their health care coverage.

The AHCA, the BCRA, and the skinny repeal bill would also have prohibited the funding of Planned Parenthood for one year, which could have had dire consequences for women of color, particularly in underserved communities. In 2014, Planned Parenthood's client base included black women at 15 percent, Latinas at 23 percent, and AAPI women at 4 percent. And in the same year, approximately 60 percent of its clients used Medicaid as their primary form of health insurance. While some conservatives insist that community health centers can absorb Planned Parenthood's clients, the reality is that many women would lose their only source of health care, because many community health centers are under-resourced and often struggle to meet the needs of their current patient loads. In addition, the proposed cuts to Medicaid would have had the most significant impact on women of color, as they are more likely to be covered by Medicaid. More than 31 percent of black women, 27 percent of Latinas, and 19 percent of AAPI women are currently enrolled in Medicaid. Over the next decade, the AHCA would have cut the Medicaid program by more than $800 billion, and the BCRA would have cut Medicaid by $772 billion. The majority of the coverage losses caused by the AHCA and the BCRA would have come from changes to the Medicaid program, namely by ending Medicaid expansion and implementing per capita caps. The per capita caps would have changed how Medicaid is financed by eliminating the entitlement to coverage for eligible individuals and the states' guarantee to federal matching dollars with no preset limit. Furthermore, states would have been able to impose enrollment caps or waiting lists on their programs to cut spending. Cuts to the program would have left millions of low-income women of color and their families without health coverage, impeding access to a wide range of services, from preventive care to treatment of chronic conditions such as diabetes, mental health, and maternity care.

The AHCA and the BCRA would not have changed the requirement for coverage of preventive care, but states would have had the ability to opt out of offering coverage for certain essential health benefits. As a result, states could have dropped certain services such as maternity care or mental health care. According to CAP estimates, a woman could have paid as much as $17,320 for a maternity services rider if these bare-bones policies had been allowed into the marketplace.

Both the AHCA and the BCRA would have allowed states to impose work requirements as a condition of Medicaid coverage with specific exceptions, such as new mothers for the first 60 days postpartum. If states were to choose this option, new mothers enrolled in Medicaid would have to return to work after 60 days or meet another exception in order to remain enrolled. This requirement would have reinforced harmful stereotypes that stigmatize mothers of color by questioning their work ethic and perpetuating the false narrative that they are engaged in fraud or abuse of the system. For example, Kelleyanne Conway, the counselor to President Donald Trump, indicated that those on Medicaid who lost health insurance could always get a job, as if they do not already work. Eighty percent of adults enrolled in Medicaid are members of working families and a majority of them work themselves. This work requirement is rooted in racial and class bias about women on Medicaid and lacks an understanding of the realities of the nation's working poor.

Finally, the AHCA and the BCRA would have imposed sweeping restrictions on insurance coverage of abortion, banning abortion beyond the Hyde Amendment exceptions. Hyde is the budgetary rider that prevents federal funds from paying for abortion care except in cases of rape, incest, or endangering the life of the mother. The AHCA would have allowed states to continue to regulate fully insured plans, but states would have been limited to using federal tax credits to purchase plans that did not cover abortion. The AHCA would have banned qualified health plans in the marketplace from covering abortion beyond the Hyde restrictions. It also would have prevented small employers from receiving tax credits if their plans covered abortion.

And unlike the AHCA, the BCRA would have banned abortion coverage beyond the Hyde restrictions in all marketplace plans, essentially preventing states from regulating their own insurance plans. Tax credits could not have been used to purchase private plans that included abortion coverage. The BCRA also attached the Hyde Amendment to the State Stability and Innovation Program, a new fund that was part of the BCRA and aimed to lower premiums or encourage insurer participation in the individual market. Therefore, plans that cover abortion would not have been eligible to receive payments from this fund.

Conclusion

Women of color need comprehensive health care—not just to protect their health but also to protect their economic security. The recent failure of the ACA repeal effort signals the need for a bipartisan effort in the Senate to improve health care. Congress should expand Medicaid, fully fund Title X and Planned Parenthood, and work to close the remaining coverage gap.

Women of color would have been made more vulnerable had any of the ACA repeal or replace bills passed into law. Repeal would make it extremely difficult to reduce the health care disparities that plague women of color and to ensure that they have the support they need to be healthy and economically stable.

VIEWPOINT 4

> "...[The] stigma against PPD in the U.S. is lessening in part because celebrities such as Brooke Shields have gone public about their own PPD."

Stigma Hinders Treatment for Postpartum Depression

Joanne Silberner

In this viewpoint, Joanne Silberner explains how stigma is the main cause of untreated postpartum depression (PPD). Most women who show signs of PPD do not get the help they need because of shame and guilt. Moreover, many healthcare providers are not trained for PPD. Insurance companies do not routinely cover PPD treatments either. In Uganda, PPD treatments are facilitated because postpartum depression is dissociated with the term "mental illness." Women there are able to get the help and support they need because PPD is labeled "the worries," as opposed to depression. Joanne Silberner is a multimedia reporter who covered health policy, global health and other health-related issues for NPR for 18 years.

As you read, consider the following questions:

1. What are some of the symptoms of postpartum depression?

"Stigma Hinders Treatment for Postpartum Depression," by Joanne Silberner, NPR.org and The Rosalynn Carter Fellowship for Mental Health Journalism, August 1, 2011. Reprinted by permission.

2. What is the difference between PPD and "baby blues?"
3. Why is postpartum depression called "the worries" in Uganda?

When Heidi Koss picks up her daughter Bronwen from middle school in a Seattle suburb, it's completely routine: They chat about kickball and whether Bronwen ate the muffin her mother packed for a snack.

But 10 years ago when Bronwen was born, things were anything but ordinary, says Koss.

"I felt nothing toward my baby," says Koss. "One day I woke up and I didn't care about her."

Koss was going through postpartum depression, or PPD, thought to be caused by a combination of stress, genetics and hormonal changes. It was her second time; she'd also had it after the birth of her first daughter, Elora. Surveys show that 1 in 7 new mothers in the U.S. have a prolonged period of overwhelming depression or anxiety after giving birth.

PPD is different from the "baby blues," a term for the temporary sadness that can hit women right after birth for a few days or a few weeks. PPD lasts for months and bears a special stigma that makes it more difficult for mothers to get care, not just in the U.S. but in other parts of the world as well.

Symptoms can include changes in sleep or weight or activity levels, intense anxiety and a lack of interest in life. One study shows that half of women with PPD have obsessions, like thoughts of hurting their babies.

On The Brink of Suicide

Koss had those violent thoughts, and they drove her to attempt suicide. Her husband pulled her back from a third-floor window ledge. She held a knife to her wrist. And at one point, she lined up a lethal dose of pills.

The only thing that that kept her from suicide was her conviction that no one would love her baby as much as she did, and no one would take care of her as well.

Her profound unhappiness was hard for her to admit at the time. "I felt like admitting that I was struggling meant I was a bad mother, so I kind of put on my best face and best foot forward and soldiered on," she says.

She eventually went to her obstetrician, but he said there was nothing much he could do. Then Koss found a support group, now known as Postpartum Support International, 17 months after Elora was born. After Bronwen was born, Koss got treatment, and while she still suffered symptoms, she says that with the help of the support group, she didn't feel so alone.

Katherine Wisner, a professor of psychiatry at the University of Pittsburgh who's been studying postpartum depression since 1985, says it's hard to get doctors interested in PPD. She says many are not trained for it, and insurance companies often don't reimburse for it.

But, she says, treatment, which consists of counseling or antidepressants, can help about half the time, and acknowledging the disease can at least ease the social strain.

Mothers from all socioeconomic groups are affected. In a recent survey of 10,000 women who had given birth at a University of Pittsburgh hospital, Wisner and her colleagues found that 14 percent across all economic classes showed symptoms that met the criteria for PPD.

PPD in Uganda

And PPD occurs outside the U.S., too. Take, for example, Uganda, a country whose government has made access to mental health care a new priority.

In a 1983 paper in the journal Social Psychiatry, Scottish psychiatrist John Cox looked at 18 women in Uganda with PPD. He reported that the women were unlikely to seek medical care for their condition, and that their symptoms were similar to those in Scottish women, except for one thing: The Ugandan women felt less guilty about their PPD.

One reason may be that many were never aware of exactly what they had. Psychiatrist Florence Baingana—one of about 30 psychiatrists in Uganda—says there isn't much awareness about PPD as a mental illness. "If it isn't recognized as a mental disorder, the stigma may not be attached to it," she says. The downside is that many cases are likely to go undiagnosed and untreated. The upside is that women are more willing to be treated.

That's what happened with 30-year-old Dorothy Mwesiga, who lives in a small village. Mwesiga had symptoms of PPD after all three of her babies were born.

Sometimes she would just sit, unable to do anything other than feel anxious. She says she felt like she was losing her mind and was terrified someone would take her babies away. "After the first time, I was frightened," she said. "But I thought it would be the end of it."

Mwesiga got help from a local nurse, Emmanuel Musumba, who like most other health officers across Uganda, has gotten some psychiatric training from the government. He treated her with antidepressant drugs and talk therapy, and she got better. But Mwesiga was never told she had PPD; instead Musumba told her she had "the worries."

Treating "The Worries"

Her husband, a driver for the pastor of the local church, has been enormously supportive, she says, and so have her relatives and neighbors. But Musumba says that wouldn't be the case if they thought she had a mental illness.

"In Africa," he says, "depression is not easy to explain. I told her I was treating the worries, and that all would be well if she took the medication."

Mwesiga's only worry now is that she will run out of free medication provided by the government before her depression ends. It happens often, he says.

Koss, the American woman with PPD, went on to get a master's degree and a license as a mental health practitioner. She counsels women about PPD and is active with the support group Postpartum Support International.

She thinks the stigma against PPD in the U.S. is lessening in part because celebrities such as Brooke Shields have gone public about their own PPD. "I now feel comfortable talking about it," Koss says. "There's not as much shame."

Viewpoint 5

> *"In so many overt or covert ways, workplace conversations are heavily loaded against pregnant women, and are met with groans, visible or invisible, by bosses, including female ones."*

Pregnant Employees Must Not Be Seen as a Liability

Rasheeda Bhagat

In the following viewpoint Rasheeda Bhagat argues that women should not be penalized for having to take maternity leave when pregnant. SBI, India's largest bank, released new guidelines for their recruiting approach, labeling pregnant prospects as "temporarily unfit." It generated a public backlash, with the Chairperson of the Delhi Commission for Women having to weigh in as well. Bhagat explains that, though the absence of an employee for a period of time can be a temporary inconvenience, bringing a child into the world is not a small affair. Therefore, pregnant employees should not be seen as a liability to companies. Rasheeda Bhagat is a writer and editor at the Hindu Business Line.

As you read, consider the following questions:

1. Why did the author believe that SBI failed to be gender-correct when they withdrew the new guidelines?

"Pregnant Employees Must Not Be Seen as a Liability," by Rasheeda Bhagat, The Hindu Business Line, February 7, 2022. Reprinted by permission.

2. Who is Charlotte Bellis?
3. Why couldn't she stay in Qatar, and why couldn't she go back to New Zealand?

India's largest bank was in the news recently, not for some huge defaulter scooting overseas, but for its recent communication on revised recruitment norms. Under the new rules which had been formulated, a woman candidate, who is more than three months pregnant, will be considered "temporarily unfit" to join duty. Magnanimously, it had added such a woman candidates could join duty within four months after delivery!

Expectedly there was a largescale public outcry and the Chairperson of the Delhi Commission for Women, Swati Maliwal, tweeted terming the bank's move both "discriminatory and illegal, as it could affect maternity benefits provided under the law."

SBI quickly withdrew the new guidelines, but failed to be gender-correct, saying that these new rules were kept in abeyance in "view of public sentiment." The statement also talked about "some sections of the media" interpreting the revised guidelines "discriminatory against women." The wording makes it abundantly clear that whoever had thought of this devious way of keeping out a section of women, resented the recall of the revised guidelines.

Of course some noise had to be made about how this mammoth bank is conscious of gender equity, so the press note added that SBI has always been proactive in the "care and empowerment of its women employees, who now constitute about 25 per cent of our workforce." It also pointed out that during the Covid pandemic, according to government instructions, pregnant employees were exempted from attending office and allowed to work from home.

Apparently, in the present scheme of things, women candidates up to six months pregnant are allowed to join the bank, provided they get a medical certificate saying that taking up employment at this state of pregnancy would not affect her health.

The distressing part about this whole brouhaha is that too often a pregnant employee or new entrant is seen as a liability. In so many overt or covert ways, workplace conversations are heavily loaded against pregnant women, and are met with groans, visible or invisible, by bosses, including female ones.

Of course, the absence, or impending absence, of your star performer from the workplace for a period of time is an inconvenience. But then miracles, like bringing a child into this world, don't happen just like that.

Thankfully, both governments and employers have stepped up their support for new mothers, by increasing maternity leave and expanding its scope by allowing paternity leave too. So the new mother can return to work sooner, knowing that at least one parent is home to take care of the baby.

There is no doubt that quicker return to work after childbirth helps to stop the disruption or stagnation in a woman's career and we owe it to one half of our population, who unfortunately do not make up one half of our workforce in the organised sector, to give their best to their organisations.

Bizarre Case

When the discussion is about pregnancy and supporting pregnant women, we have to talk about the bizarre case of Charlotte Bellis, a pregnant Kiwi journalist working for Al Jazeera, who was struggling to return home as her application had got entangled in New Zealand's very strict MIQ (managed isolated quarantine) rules for everyone returning to the country from a foreign land.

Telling her story in the New Zealand Herald, she says that after being told for years by doctors that she can never conceive a child, she found herself pregnant while in Qatar. Her partner is a freelance photographer who works for the The New York Times.

The problem is that in Qatar the law doesn't allow an unmarried woman to be pregnant. He is from Belgium and the Schengen visa rules allowed her to stay only for a few months and she didn't have health insurance either.

As her attempt to get back to her home country got frustrated by the MIQ quotas and other technicalities, she had to ironically turn to the Taliban, for Afghanistan was the only country for which both the journalists had valid visas. Even more ironic, Charlotte was the journalist who had asked the Taliban at its maiden press conference after taking over the country, on how it would treat the Afghan women!

Well, fact is often stranger than fiction. According to her column, the Taliban, which publicly lashes Afghan women for even going out with an unrelated man, gave them permission to return to Afghanistan, advising them to tell everybody that they were married.

But she was terrified at the prospect of delivering her baby in a country with poor medical facilities.

But fortunately, after much dilly-dallying, the New Zealand government has now facilitated Charlotte's return to her home country to deliver her child in a safe environment. This has thankfully put an end to her trauma.

Viewpoint 6

> *"Research proves that there are certainly challenges that are systemic among women from a health perspective. And these problems don't exist in the male physiology, like a period cycle every month, for example."*

Period Leave Can Help Women in the Workforce

Surekha Ragavan

Recently, a few companies in India and the Asia-Pacific region have started adding period leave as part of their benefits. It's part of an effort to destigmatize menstrual periods. Many women suffer from severe period pain. In addition, the stigma related to a period is based on cultural and religious beliefs. Women are considered impure when they have their period and are sometimes banned from certain religious and social practices. Offering period leave was a way for companies to acknowledge the health challenges that women face and to promote inclusivity in the organization. Those changes have brought on positive changes for those companies. Surekha Ragavan is a writer and editor for Campaign Asia and PRWeek Asia.

As you read, consider the following questions:

1. Why does the author believe that a period leave should not be classified as a sick day?

"Period Leave: A Privilege or a Basic Right?" by Surekha Ragavan, Campaign Asia, March 8, 2021. Reprinted by permission.

2. What are some of the arguments against period leave?
3. What are some of the evident impacts that the author cited in this viewpoint?

People who menstruate are often familiar with the tiptoed act they put on in the workplace. Going to the bathroom "discreetly" armed with their sanitary product woe betide a colleague spots them holding it; the mild pang of "fear" every time they sneeze or stand up; an inconspicuous glance at their chair to see if they've left a stain; and the agony of cramps in the middle of a meeting.

To create a more equitable workplace, some companies have introduced period leave where those who menstruate are eligible to take a day off each month to recover without it being taken out of their sick days. This, in essence, doesn't just allow staff time to recuperate if they need to, but it also puts the subject of periods on the table—a topic that has long been stigmatised in this part of the world. So much so that slang terms such as "time of the month," "surfing the crimson wave" or "having the painters in" have become accepted jargon in the workplace to refer to periods.

M&C Saatchi Australia is a rare agency in this region to introduce period leave for staff who menstruate. When general manager Nathalie Brady and her team asked staff about benefits that they wished for, the creative department sparked the idea of period leave. And when it was finally implemented and announced, Brady said "you could just hear the cheers around the office from women."

She told Campaign Asia-Pacific that implementing period leave was a gesture to empathise with staff and let them know that it can be difficult during those days, and that there's no shame in asking for time off.

"Some women suffer from horrendous conditions like endometriosis and fibroids that really impact them on a monthly

Reproductive Rights

> ## Menstruation Is Stigmatized in Many Countries
>
> Each day, some 800 million people between the ages of 15 - 49 are menstruating. Yet for so many, a natural biological process spells more than a monthly inconvenience.
>
> In some countries, menstruation is taboo or riddled with myths, and women and girls are excluded from daily activities because of stigma, shame or discrimination or because they are considered unclean. In others, menarche may lead to child marriage or sexual violence because it signals a girl is ready for motherhood or sexual activity. Girls may miss school because they do not have access to sanitary supplies, they are in pain or their schools lack adequate sanitary facilities. Some girls do not understand what's happening to their bodies. And more than 26 million women and girls are estimated to be displaced because of conflict or climate disaster, robbing them of dignity when they have difficulty managing their periods and exacerbating their vulnerability.
>
> While some countries have addressed period poverty, or the hardship of affording menstrual products, more can be done, especially in normalizing something 1.9 billion people of reproductive age do— girls, women, transgender men and nonbinary people. Menstruation should not mean the end of rights to health, dignity and gender equality.
>
> "Menstrual Health," United Nations Population Fund.

basis," said Brady. "You know that feeling when you're having a heavy period, and you're in the middle of a meeting—everyone's had those awful moments. Let's not underestimate the amount of stress and anxiety that comes with. If you're not a woman, or if you don't experience that, you don't understand what that's like."

"Why Not Just Take It out of Your Sick Day?"

Period leave has been a contentious issue in the region with many arguing that it should be classified as a sick day. But lumping period-related time off under sick days comes with issues: Firstly, if a company requires a doctor's note to justify a sick day, this means that staff will be forced to consult a doctor whenever they need time off to recover from cramps or heavy bleeding.

Brady argued that separating period leave from sick days is also a symbol of equitability. "Research proves that there are certainly challenges that are systemic among women from a health perspective. And these problems don't exist in the male physiology, like a period cycle every month, for example," she said.

"And so, it feels equitable for women to have a slight benefit in leave for the [health] challenges that they have to go through. And on the flip side, we look to be equally as equitable for men when it comes to having children. We have equal pay parental leave for both mothers and fathers."

At Indian digital marketing company Culture Machine, providing period leave outside of sick days meant destigmatising periods as a "sickness" or something "dirty." "This is something that happens to women naturally, it's how your body functions," said Reema D'souza, assistant HR manager at Culture Machine. "We wanted people to be upfront and open about it."

HR staff at Culture Machine decided to implement period leave because they had noticed that some staff who menstruate would take a sick day each month while being vague about their symptoms, and the company realised that this "trend" was due to a fear of telling managers about period pain. "The idea of period leave for us was to make it comfortable for women to take the leap without feeling ashamed to walk up to their male or female managers," said D'souza.

In India, the stigma around menstruation runs deep, supplemented by religious and cultural practices. When on their period, women are often considered "impure" and are excluded from social and religious events. They are also denied entry into some places of worship, and in more conservative communities, disallowed to step into their kitchens. On top of that, access to sanitary products remains a major issue. So something as seemingly inconsequential as period leave is a big step forward to removing some of those barriers, and might just aid in raising awareness around systemic inequity that have led many Indian women to suffer in silence.

But it's not always the case where period leave is accepted with open arms. Last year, Indian delivery platform Zomato introduced period leave for all menstruating staff, and a memo to staff penned by founder and CEO Deepinder Goyal was made public. The memo included a note to men: "Our female colleagues expressing that they are on their period leave shouldn't be uncomfortable for us. This is a part of life, and while we don't fully understand what women go through, we need to trust them when they say they need to rest."

Zomato's decision sparked a divisive nationwide debate on social media with many—both men and women—calling the move as "unequal" and "backward." Some argued that period leave may "push women out of decision-making roles at offices." One reporter on Twitter said "Sorry Zomato, as woke as your decision on #PeriodLeave is, this is exactly what ghettoizes women and strengthens biological determinism."

Feminist activists in India, on the other hand, argued that women claiming that periods are "not a big deal" risked invalidating the stress and pain many who menstruate do endure. One woman said on Twitter: "Period experiences are different for different women and no one person can speak for all. Those who suffer from extreme forms of it, and have for years, we didn't choose this. The burden of not being discriminated against should not be on us."

M&C Saatchi Australia too was—to some extent—berated after publicising their policy. The comments beneath this story indicate that many still think of period leave as the "opposite of empowerment" or "belittling to women" and a "personal matter that should be kept internally."

The Evident Impact of Period Leave

For Emperikal, a digital marketing agency based in Kuala Lumpur, period leave has greatly improved staff morale in the company. Saiful Amir Omar, principal consultant and founder of the agency, said that because periods usually happen once a month, the company decided to "acknowledge the science" and ease the process for menstruating staff. And this showed to have an effect on staff productivity.

"Goodwill is reciprocal," said Omar. "We have understanding that everyone who feels heard and understood are more likely to perform over the expected goals when they are in good condition."

Because menstrual cycles are something that can be estimated, the teams at Emperikal said that they know when and how to manage this, and are able to delegate effectively during peak business periods. Internal HR data from the agency obtained by Campaign Asia-Pacific showed that since period leave was implemented, the number of short notice leave and sick days taken by female staff reduced significantly from 9 days to 1.1 days across three years.

Menstruating staff at the agency also provided accounts of how period leave has impacted them. One associate art director said: "It's definitely great to get a day off when your menses are killing you. I feel like all companies should have it because no women can focus and deal with menstrual pain at the same time."

One copywriter said: "It helps people with more serious symptoms feel less bad about their bodies at the workplace so that's a pretty neat thing. It's also a good inclusivity practice. Knowing menstrual leave is on the table means that the company values menstruators and is more likely a welcoming place for people who menstruate like women and other marginalised genders, which is kind of cool."

And one senior account manager added: "A lot of employers think that employees are trying to cheat them to get more 'holidays.' Companies need to understand that it is a natural cycle, and that all women go through this together but in their own unique ways. Personally, I have my moments with cramps so I don't take the leave consistently, but I think it is great to have because I have a lot of friends who suffer terrible cramps."

Interestingly, because Emperikal has been public about its period leave policy, it has also aided in getting more women to apply for roles at the agency. HR data showed that the ratio of females to males in job applications increased from 10:90 to 60:40 within three years of the agency implementing period leave.

"It helps to remove 'selection bias' among candidates because menstruation is something that the company acknowledges to be part of the norm rather than a disadvantage when hiring female employees compared to male candidates," said Michelle Ding, director of creative content at Emperikal." And we have seen that having this as part of a company benefit really allows us to reach out to a wider female creative talent pool."

VIEWPOINT 7

| *"The moment we gender our leave policies, we gender our assignments."*

Women Should Not Be Entitled to Menstrual Leave

Radhika Santhanam

In this interview moderated by Radhika Santhanam, Barkha Dutt and Kavita Krishnan explain both sides of the argument on period leave. Krishnan offers her take on why period leave could be a positive step toward change, and Dutt gives a fuller view of why many feminists opposed the company Zomato's announcement on a new paid menstrual leave policy. Dutt believes that the gendered nature of this policy will hurt women in the long run because women have to fight twice as hard as men to be recognized for their efforts in the workforce. Kavita Krishnan is CPI (ML) Politburo member, and Secretary, All India Progressive Women's Association. Barkha Dutt is senior journalist and Editor of Mojo.

As you read, consider the following questions:

1. If a woman needs to take a sick day for period pain, what type of paid leave does Barkha Dutt believe it should fall under?
2. How many girls drop out of school after reaching puberty in India?

"Should Women be Entitled to Menstrual Leave?" by Radhika Santhanam, The Hindu, August 21, 2020. Reprinted by permission.

3. Why does Barkha Dutt believe that period leave policies will shut the door on women?

Last week, Zomato announced a new paid menstrual leave policy for its employees, 35% of whom are women. While this is not the first time that a company is announcing such a policy, it has triggered a sharp debate among women themselves on whether this is a progressive move, mere tokenism, or a regressive move. Barkha Dutt and Kavita Krishnan discuss the issue in a conversation moderated by Radhika Santhanam. Edited excerpts:

Barkha, you tweeted that you are opposed to this policy. Zomato is granting 10 days of leave, and whether women avail it or don't is up to them; it is a choice. So, why do you think this is a bad idea?

Barkha Dutt: My opposition does not come from the number of days that Zomato has announced; it comes more from what I believe this policy represents. I have had to fight to go on certain assignments, to be assigned certain kinds of stories. I know how tilted newsrooms are towards the casual hierarchical supremacy of men. Women have had to fight twice as hard to get to the same place as men. Because I am inherently opposed to the gendering of the workplace, I see period leave as the gendering of the workplace, as a statement of biological determinism, as using biology against women to offer equal opportunities and assignments.

In the nature-versus-nurture debate, I have always been on the side of nurture. I believe that social differences and constructs create our differences, not biological essentialism. And I believe period leave is biological essentialism that my feminism opposes.

But don't you think workplaces should be designed taking into consideration the needs of women rather than ignoring them?

Barkha Dutt: Your question presupposes that it is the need of all women to have a day off. If a woman has a particularly debilitating period, if she has endometriosis or is in a situation where she can't work, I believe that should qualify under the larger bracket of medical leave.

I have a problem with all women being generalised as women needing menstrual leave. And if the argument against that is that it cuts into normally assigned medical leave, I do not have a problem if medical leave is extended for both women and men for extenuating circumstances a couple of times a month; leave that a man is also entitled to for different problems that we can't identify. I have a problem with biology-specified medical leave.

Kavita, do you think there should be separate menstrual leave or should women just avail of medical leave if they are unable to go to work?

Kavita Krishnan: I understand and empathise with what Barkha is saying. As women who work in a world which is extremely unfair in so many ways, it is a double bind for many women. Women I have spoken to have asked, do we assert our pain and emotional states around the time of our period or will doing so mean that we are conforming to the patriarchal notion that women are not the same as men or not as good as men?

I would like to understand this as a fundamental issue of the relationship between gloriously diverse human bodies and social selves and the world of work. Should workplaces be shaped only for an abstract and one-size-fits-all capitalism or should they be shaped keeping in mind the optimum productivity and comfort of diverse human bodies and selves?

This is a debate that we've been having since the 19th century. The debate has been brought up not just in the context of women, but even when it came to the human right to sleep; for an eight-hour workday; for weekends; for bathroom breaks; for food breaks—all these are seen as time stolen from the labour time that the capitalist has bought. I feel that places of work should be reshaped to acknowledge these social divisions and that will help people be more productive.

Also, I am not at all in favour of medicalising menstruation. I don't think this is about a medical issue, about debilitating pain. It is about our being differently productive around those times and our being able to avail of those differently productive times.

Could you elaborate on how we should reshape workplaces for diverse bodies and selves?

Kavita Krishnan: Let me quote the anthropologist Emily Martin here: "Women are perceived as malfunctioning and their hormones [as] out of balance, rather than seeing the organization of society and work perceived in need of a transformation to demand less constant and disciplined productivity of a certain kind."

So, the idea is that women are more creative around their period, whereas meeting deadlines and doing certain kinds of work may not be what those particular women choose to do at the time. And this is about women, menstruating people, people with a variety of different abilities and disabilities. Let me give you a simple example: we say ramps should be in places so that people with wheelchairs are able to access these places. Would that be biological determinism? Would we say then that biology is coming in the way of equality?

Barkha Dutt: I see Kavita's point about diverse selves and the relationship between diverse selves and workplace. And if that is the conversation, if the conversation was not so gendered, I would have been a lot more comfortable with it. I would have been comfortable with the conversation being about easy access to sanitary pads or separate bathrooms—20% of Indian girls drop out of school after reaching puberty, according to the United Nations. And in large part this happens because of the stigma that continues to exist in large parts of the country around menstruation. So, the conversations

What Reproductive Health Concerns Do Women Face?

I want to have are about destigmatising menstruation, diversity at the workplace, access to sanitary pads or menstrual cups, why religious orthodoxy looks at menstruation as impure, etc.

If I am a woman fighting to have women as infantry soldiers in the military, and we have a gendered leave policy, can we as women ask to be soldiers on the front-lines? Can we ask to be deployed in conflict zones? The moment we gender our leave policies, we gender our assignments.

Weren't these the same arguments that were used even when women fought for maternity leave? That they wouldn't be able to do certain jobs? But feminists fought for it.

Barkha Dutt: Which is why my battle is for parenting leave. There are people who adopt children and that relationship is also no less. If we are truly evolved, we should encourage the same kind of leave for men.

Yes, but parenting does involve the participation of men and women, whereas only women get their period.

Barkha Dutt: So, even if I have no problem during my period, I should get leave because it is specific to my biology? Even if I have no pain, nothing? Parenting is not the same thing as our monthly period. Even our notions of maternity leave are evolving. The most involved organisations have family leave. If there is no equality at home, there is no equality at work. And if we place the responsibility of parenting entirely on women, through some romantic notion of how our biological differences make us different from men, we confirm stereotypes.

Kavita Krishnan: But we are different. There are biological differences, and not just between men and women. If someone requires a wheelchair, we would expect the workplace to be designed to ensure that that person is able to access the workplace and be their best there. People in wheelchairs will be told they can't do certain jobs. But would we accept that? No, we should be able to redesign workplaces so that all of us can access those spaces. My arguments are not just about gendered differences. My arguments are that workers in all their diversity need workplaces to acknowledge how they are treated.

And let me tell you, period leave in India isn't some fancy thing that Zomato has just introduced. In Bihar, government employees have availed of it since the 1990s. They asked for it, got it and have been quietly availing of it since then. We went and asked them about their experiences—has it meant more discrimination, have they been treated more differently—and they argued that differential treatment happened even before they had this leave. That differential treatment requires just various excuses and this is just one excuse among men.

Barkha, you had said on Twitter that such a policy would shut the doors for women and that you would shut them too for someone who thinks this is a good time to take off. Do you still stand by that?

Barkha Dutt: I think my comment has been totally misrepresented. I do believe many doors will shut for women with a generalised period leave and I believe that someone like me would no longer be able to argue that all jobs and all roles should be kept open for women. Think once again about reporting or fighting war or going into space. It is not because I don't report on what could be unique female experiences. During my four months on the road reporting COVID-19 for example, one of my reports was the story of a female nurse and her experience bleeding in a PPE. I also had my period twice while wearing a PPE inside a COVID-19 hospital and it was a traumatic experience but nothing that would make me step back from the chance of reporting that very story with all its difficulties. Again, to repeat, once we start accepting the specificity of gender, it weakens our argument against gender barriers. Let us talk in more general, less-gendered terms of an inclusive, equal work space.

Kavita Krishnan: I would also like to respond to this. Any demand for equality and dignity at work has been a pretext for shutting the door on women. For that matter, even men availing of parental leave are subjected to discrimination. The idea that women demanding or availing of period leave should/would be sacked is much like the idea that women complaining of sexual harassment at work should/would be sacked, or would not be hired.

Isn't it a biological stereotype to assume that menstruating bodies (or bodies needing wheelchairs) be treated exactly as bodies that do not menstruate or need wheelchairs? I think gender blindness does not bring gender equality. Rather, being blind to gender diversity (and other bodily and social diversities) leads workplaces to be wilfully blind to the various kinds of gender and social discriminations.

Kavita, since you think that period leave should be given, what do you think is the ideal number of days? Do you see this being implemented in the near future?

Kavita Krishnan: I don't think I or anyone can suggest an "ideal" number of days for period leave. We are in times when employees and workers are having to struggle to defend and implement every single labour law. Even maternity leave and benefits are mostly implemented only where there are unions to fight for implementation. Otherwise, the laws are flouted by employers. The same holds for period leave.

Reproductive Rights

Periodical and Internet Sources Bibliography

The following articles have been selected to supplement the diverse views presented in this chapter.

"A fresh look at paternity leave: Why the benefits extend beyond the personal," McKinsey & Company, March 5, 2021. https://www.mckinsey.com/business-functions/people-and-organizational-performance/our-insights/a-fresh-look-at-paternity-leave-why-the-benefits-extend-beyond-the-personal

BBC, "Spain plans menstrual leave in new law for those with severe pain," BBC, May 13, 2022. https://www.bbc.com/news/world-europe-61429022

Mindy Christianson, M.D., "Period pain: Could it be endometriosis?" John Hopkins Medicine, n.d. https://www.hopkinsmedicine.org/health/wellness-and-prevention/period-pain-could-it-be-endometriosis

Julia Dennison, "Why new dads should take paternity leave," n.d. https://www.parents.com/pregnancy/my-life/maternity-paternity-leave/why-new-dads-should-take-paternity-leave/

Katie Dimond, "Period poverty and the pandemic: a forgotten crisis," Columbia University, May 4, 2022. https://www.publichealth.columbia.edu/public-health-now/news/period-poverty-and-pandemic-forgotten-crisis

Áine Doris, "What happened when a US state scrapped the 'tampon tax'," Chicago Booth Review, March 23, 2021. https://www.chicagobooth.edu/review/what-happened-when-us-state-scrapped-tampon-tax

Deborah D'Souza, "Tampon Tax," Investopia, September 30, 2021. https://www.investopedia.com/tampon-tax-4774993

Mayo Clinic Staff, "Postpartum depression," Mayo Clinic, n.d. https://www.mayoclinic.org/diseases-conditions/postpartum-depression/symptoms-causes/syc-20376617

Oyster Team, "Parental leave in France: The nuts and bolts of paternity and maternity leave in France," Oyster, September 7, 2021. https://www.oysterhr.com/library/parental-leave-in-france

Leah Rodriguez, "The tampon tax: everything you need to know," Global Citizen, June 28, 2021. https://www.globalcitizen.org/en/content/tampon-tax-explained-definition-facts-statistics/

For Further Discussion

Chapter 1
1. Kimberley Brownlee quotes Judith Jarvis Thomson's essay "A Defense of Abortion." Do you agree or disagree with Thomson's Good Samaritan argument? Explain your answer.
2. In his argument, Paul Stark stresses that abortion is not a gender issue. How does he support his argument? Does it seem like a valid argument? Explain your answer.
3. Marcus Lee argues that the men's rights activists' movement comes from an anti-Black ethos. Do you agree with this assertion? Why or why not?

Chapter 2
1. Maureen Miller's argument asserts that Planned Parenthood is becoming increasingly crucial to men as well. How does she support this argument? Do you agree or disagree with her? Explain your answer.
2. Alexandra DeSanctis uses four arguments to make her case against Planned Parenthood. What does she bring forth as evidence? Do you find her arguments convincing?
3. Laura McGuire asserts that preventing sexual misconduct starts with education that shifts the paradigms and norms people have about sex, relationships, and bodily autonomy. How does she support her argument? Explain.

Chapter 3
1. Why are issues surrounding IVF and surrogacy rights most often relegated to women? Would these rights be more fair if men were also considered connected to reproductive rights?
2. Naomi Cahn and Sonia Suter argue that, even though the new donor identity laws might increase the cost of fertility treatment, genetic testing might not add much to the cost

Reproductive Rights

because it would only be done once, rather than each time a patient obtains a vial of sperm. Do you agree with their assessment? Why or why not?
3. Do you think gamete donation should move more toward an open-identity system, or do you think it is best kept as anonymous? Explain your reasoning.

Chapter 4

1. Heidi Williamson believes that women of color will be the most harmed if the Affordable Care Act is repealed. Does she provide enough evidence to support her argument? What could be a counterargument to her assessment?
2. Does Rasheeda Bhagat provide enough evidence to support her argument that pregnant employees should not be seen as a liability? If yes, cite her arguments. If no, how would you support her argument?
3. Surekha Ragavan explains why period leave might help female employees. Radhika Santhanam offers a comprehensive counterargument as to why period leave might be a disservice to women. After reading both arguments, do you think companies should implement period leave as part of their policy? Explain your reasoning, citing from the viewpoints to support your answer.

Organizations to Contact

The editors have compiled the following list of organizations concerned with the issues debated in this book. The descriptions are derived from materials provided by the organizations. All have publications or information available for interested readers. The list was compiled on the date of publication of the present volume; the information provided here may change. Be aware that many organizations take several weeks or longer to respond to inquiries, so allow as much time as possible.

Center for Reproductive Rights

199 Water Street
New York, NY 10038
(917) 637-3600
email: info@reprorights.org
Website: https://reproductiverights.org

The Center for Reproductive Rights is a global organization composed of lawyers and advocates. It focuses protecting reproductive rights.

Guttmacher Institute

125 Maiden Lane 7th Floor
New York, NY 10038
(212) 248-1111
Website: https://www.guttmacher.org

Guttmacher is the leading research and policy organization focusing on reproductive health and rights.

National Abortion Federation

1090 Vermont Avenue, NW, Suite 1000
Washington, DC 20005
(202) 667-5881
email: naf@prochoice.org
Website: https://prochoice.org

Reproductive Rights

The National Abortion Federation is a professional association for abortion providers.

National Organization for Lesbian Rights

870 Market Street Suite 370
San Francisco CA 94102
(415) 392-6257
email: Info@NCLRights.org
Website: https://www.nclrights.org/contact-us/

The National Organization for Lesbian Rights focuses on the rights of gay, lesbian, transgender, bisexual and queer people, including reproductive rights.

National Sexual Violence Resource Center

2101 N Front Street
Governor's Plaza North, Building #2
Harrisburg, PA 17110
(717) 909-0715
email: resources@nsvrc.org
Website: https://www.nsvrc.org

The National Sexual Violence Resource Center's goal is to provide the general population with the right information to fight sexual violence.

Planned Parenthood

1225 4th Street, NE
Washington, DC 20002
(202) 347-8500
email: experience@ppmw.org
Website: https://www.plannedparenthood.org/planned-parenthood-metropolitan-washington-dc

Planned Parenthood is the largest single provider of reproductive health services, including birth control, screenings, pregnancy testing and counseling, STI testing, prenatal care, sex education, vasectomies, and abortion.

RESOLVE: The National Infertility Association

7918 Jones Branch Drive, Suite 300
McLean, VA 22102
(703) 556-7172
email: info@resolve.org
Website: https://resolve.org

RESOLVE helps people struggling with infertility gain access to care and to support and community.

SIECUS: Sex Ed for Social Change

(202) 265-2405
email: info@siecus.org
Website: https://siecus.org

SIECUS is an organization focusing on advancing sex education through advocacy, policy, and coalition building.

Verywell Health

28 Liberty St
New York, NY 10005
(212) 204-4000
email: contact@verywellhealth.com
Website: https://www.verywellhealth.com

Verywell Health is a resource offering up-to-date information on all things health-related, including reproductive health.

Bibliography of Books

Ryan T. Anderson, and Alexandra DeSanctis. *Tearing Us Apart: How Abortion Harms Everything and Solves Nothing.* Washington, DC: Regnery Publishing 2022.

Karen Blumenthal. *Jane Against the World: Roe v. Wade and the Fight for Reproductive Rights.* New York, NY: Roaring Brook Press, 2020.

Catherine Cho. *Inferno : A Memoir of Motherhood and Madness.* New York, NY: Henry Holt and Company, 2020.

Camilla Fitzsimons and Ruth Coppinger. *Repealed: Ireland's Unfinished Fight for Reproductive Rights.* London, UK: Pluto Press, 2021.

Roxane Gay, ed. *Not That Bad: Dispatches from Rape Culture.* New York, NY: Harper, 2018.

Michelle Hope. *The Girls' Guide to Sex Education: Over 100 Honest Answers to Urgent Questions about Puberty, Relationships, and Growing Up.* Rockridge Press, 2018.

Sarah Menkedick. *Ordinary Insanity: Fear and the Silent Crisis of Motherhood in America.* New York, NY: Pantheon Books, 2020.

Kathryn Kolbert. *Controlling Women: What We Must Do Now to Save Reproductive Freedom.* New York, NY: Hachette Books, 2021.

Jennifer Lang. *Consent: The New Rules of Sex Education: Every Teen's Guide to Healthy Sexual Relationships.* San Antonio, TX: Althea Press, 2018.

Zakiya Luna. *Reproductive Rights as Human Rights: Women of Color and the Fight for Reproductive Justice.* New York, NY: NYU Press, 2020.

Robin Stevenson. *My Body, My Choice : The Fight for Abortion Rights*. Victoria, BC: Orca Book Publishers, 2019.

Scott Todnem. *Sex Education for Boys: A Parent's Guide: Practical Advice on Puberty, Sex, and Relationships*. Rockridge Press, 2022.

Mary Ziegler. *Abortion and the Law in America: Roe v. Wade to the Present*. Cambridge, England: Cambridge University Press, 2020.

Mary Ziegler. *Beyond Abortion: Roe v. Wade and the Battle for Privacy*. Cambridge, MA: Harvard University Press, 2018.

Index

A

Abortion
　accessibility, 23-25
　cost, 23, 47, 141
　criminal justice, 27, 39
　exceptions to bans, 18, 20-22, 29-31, 70, 141
　legality, 15, 18-52
　legislation, 22-23, 29-32, 38-39, 44, 46, 48-50, 66
　safety of, 14, 20-24, 32, 47, 51
　stigma/harassment, 23-24, 26-27, 47
　travel for, 21-22
　unsafe abortions, 18-22, 26-27, 56, 134-135
Abstinence, 15, 77
Abusive relationships, 75, 126, 133
Adongo, Philip Baba, 88-92
Adoption, 35, 64, 86, 99
Affordable Care Act (Obamacare), 57, 68, 136-141
American Health Care Act of 2017 (AHCA), 68, 70-71, 137, 139-140
Amnesty International, 19-27

B

Barn, Gulzaar, 101-104
Better Care Reconciliation Act of 2017 (BCRA), 68, 70-71, 137, 139-140
Bhagat, Rasheeda, 148-151
Bodies as property, 37-42

Brownlee, Kimberley, 28-32

C

Cahn, Naomi, 105-110
Cancer, 64, 70, 72, 126-127, 138
Centers for Disease Control and Prevention (U.S.), 29-30, 63, 126
Childcare, cost, 122
Congress (U.S.), 38-39, 68-71, 105, 109, 137, 142
Consent, 15, 78-82
Constitution (U.S.)
　abortion, 29, 32
　Fourteenth Amendment, 33-34
　　Due Process Clause, 34
　　Equal Protection Clause, 33-34
Contraception, 19, 22, 24, 41, 56, 59, 64, 70, 75, 77, 89, 127-129, 132-135

D

Dawson, Ruth, 124-131
Democratic Party, 65-66, 68
DeSanctis, Alexandra, 62-66
Developing countries, 19, 21, 88-89
Disability, 130, 163-164
Discrimination
　abortion, 24-27
　healthcare, 23-25, 128-129
　workplace, 15, 122, 148-165
DNA testing, 107-110

| 174

Index

Dobbs v. Jackson Women's Health Organization, see Supreme Court
Dunt, Ian, 73-78
Dutt, Barkha, 159-165

E

Egg donation, 96-97, 99, 108-109, 111-114
Embryonic stem cell research, 49

F

Family planning, 14, 71-72, 133, 135
Fertility, 58, 86-118, 126
Flowers, Prudence, 43-47
Fraga, Juli, 115-118

G

Gender equality/equity, 16, 33-42, 149, 155, 160-165
Guttmacher Institute, 20, 63, 126-127

H

Hansen, Danielle Tumminio, 94-100
Hyde Amendment, 68, 70, 141

I

Immigrants, 22, 130
In vitro fertilization, 86, 97, 108, 115-118
India
    menstruation, 152-165
    surrogacy, 95, 98, 101-104
Indigenous communities, 22

K

Krishnan, Kavita, 159-165

L

Lee, Marcus, 37-42
Leong, Tracy, 124-131
LGBTQ+
    abortion, 22, 24-26, 40-41, 126-127
    discrimination, 24-26
    parenthood and pregnancy, 86, 99, 102, 104, 126-127
    reproductive health care, 124-131
    sex education, 82, 129-130

M

Marway, Herjeet, 101-104
McGuire, Laura, 79-82
Medicaid, 59, 68, 70-71, 138-142
Menstruation, 122, 152-165
Mental health/illness, 47, 51, 65, 90, 97, 122-123, 143-147
Miller, Maureen, 56-61

P

Paid parental leave, 15-16, 123, 148-151, 163, 165
Pennings, Guido, 111-114
Period leave, 152-165
Planned Parenthood, 46, 56-72, 139, 142
Planned Parenthood v. Casey, see Supreme Court
Postpartum depression (PPD), 122-123, 143-147

Poverty, 22, 43, 47, 51, 58, 130, 132-133, 142
Pregnancy
  economic impacts, 61, 132-133
  risks, 134, 138
  services, 57, 62, 64
  teenagers, 75, 127
  unintended, 132-135, 138

R

Racial/ethnic minorities
  abortion, 22, 25, 37-40, 47
  discrimination, 25
  reproductive health care, 130, 136-141
  sex education, 82
Racism, 37-40
Raes, Inez, 111-114
Ragavan, Surekha, 152-158
Rape, 22, 28-30, 79, 141
Ravelingien, An, 111-114
Religion, 14-15, 30-31, 74-75, 77, 99, 155, 163
Republican Party, 57, 62-63, 65, 68-70
Roe v. Wade, see Supreme Court
Rovner, Julie, 48-51

S

Santhanam, Radhika, 159-165
Sex education, 14-15, 19, 22, 30, 53-84, 129-130
Sexually transmitted infections/Diseases (STIs/STDs), 57-59, 62, 64, 72, 126-129, 138

Silberner, Joanne, 143-147
Slavery, 40
Sperm donation, 99, 105-114
Stark, Paul, 33-36
Substance abuse, 47, 65
Suicide, 144, 145
Supreme Court (U.S.)
  Dobbs v. Jackson Women's Health Organization, 29-32, 43-45
  Planned Parenthood v. Casey, 46
  Roe v. Wade, 15, 18, 29, 34, 43-50, 70
Surrogacy, 86, 94-104
Suter, Sonia, 105-110

T

Tabong, Philip Teg-Nefaah, 88-92
Thomson, Judith Jarvis, 28-32
Title X, 71, 142

U

United Nations
  abortion, 25
  Convention on the Elimination of All Forms of Discrimination Against Women (CEDAW), 26

V

Vance, Laurence M., 67-72

W

Williamson, Heidi, 136-142
World Health Organization (WHO), 19-23, 88-89, 101, 103, 132-135